BLOOP

Part One

Written and Drawn by Steve Conley

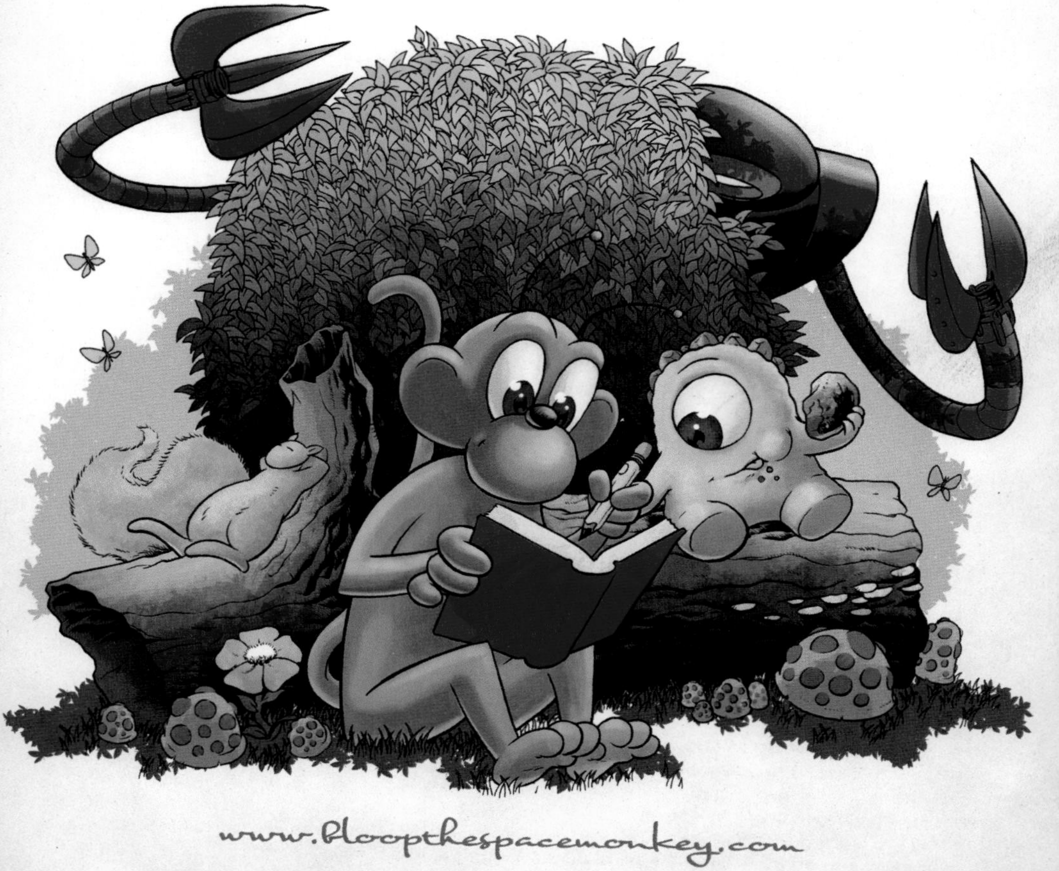

www.bloopthespacemonkey.com

Big thanks from a tiny space monkey!

YOUR SUPPORT AND KINDNESS MEAN THE WORLD TO ME...
ANDY • ART • BATTON • BETH • BRITT • CAROLYN • CHRIS
CHRISTINE • DEAN • ERIKA • FRANK • GRAHAM • JACKIE • JAMAR
JAMES • JERRY • JIMMY • JOHN • MARC • MARTY • MICHAEL • NATHAN
NICK • RICH • RICHARD • RICK • SCOTT • SHELTON • THOM

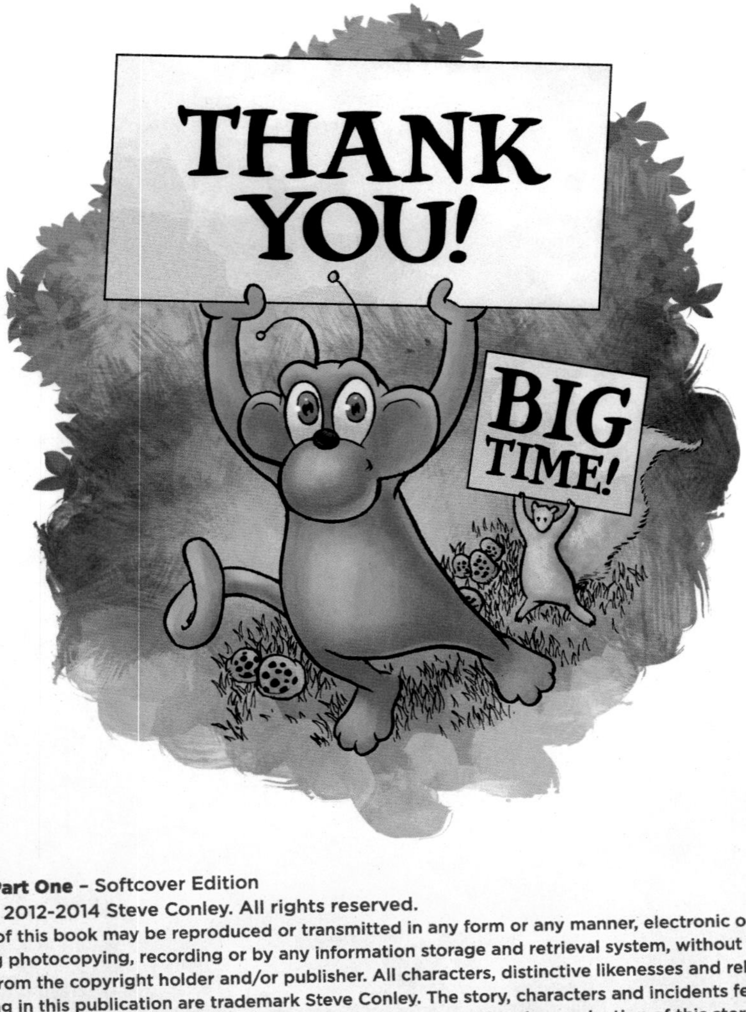
THANK YOU!
BIG TIME!

Bloop: Part One – Softcover Edition

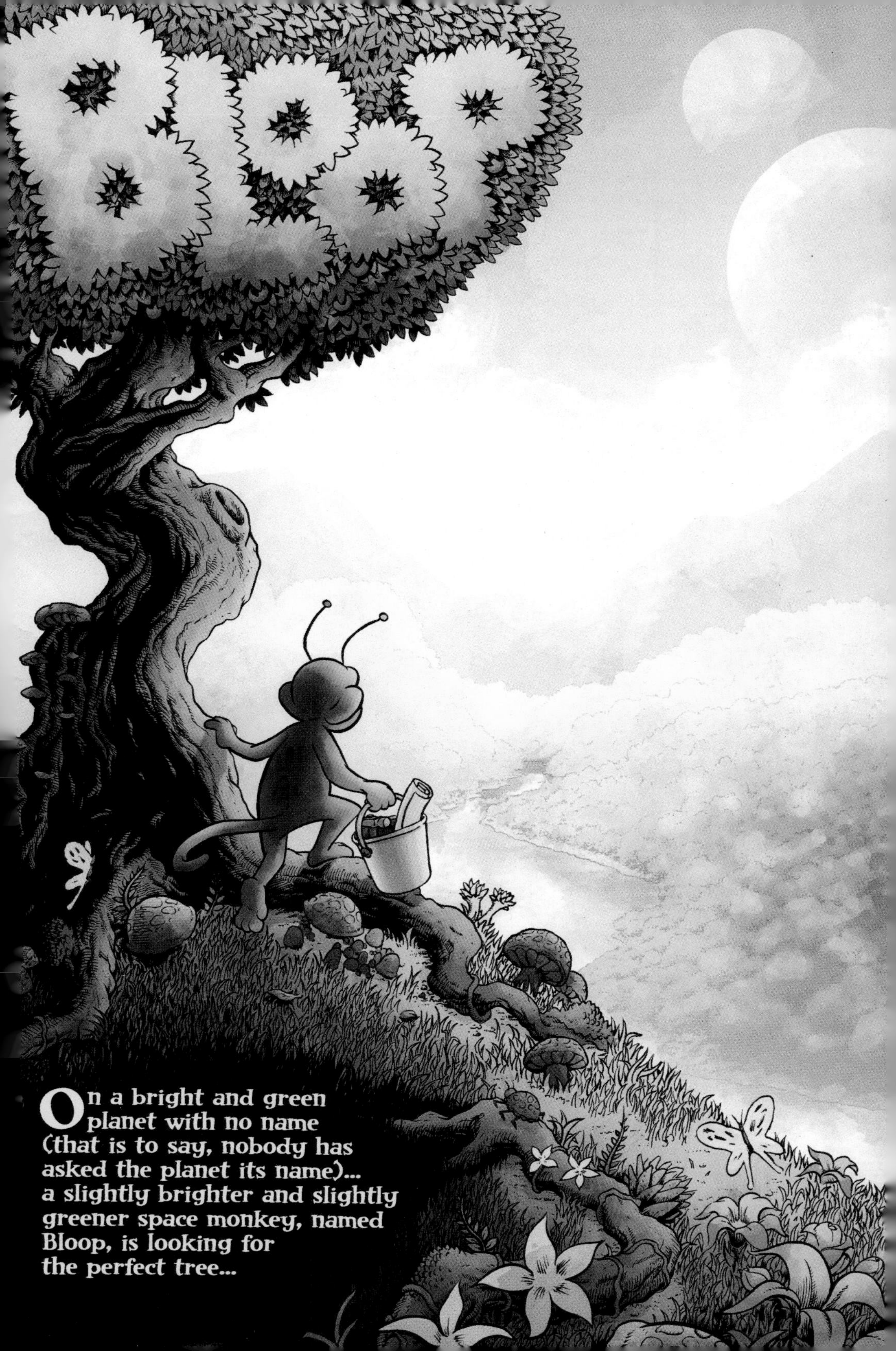
BLOOP
On a bright and green planet with no name (that is to say, nobody has asked the planet its name)... a slightly brighter and slightly greener space monkey, named Bloop, is looking for the perfect tree...

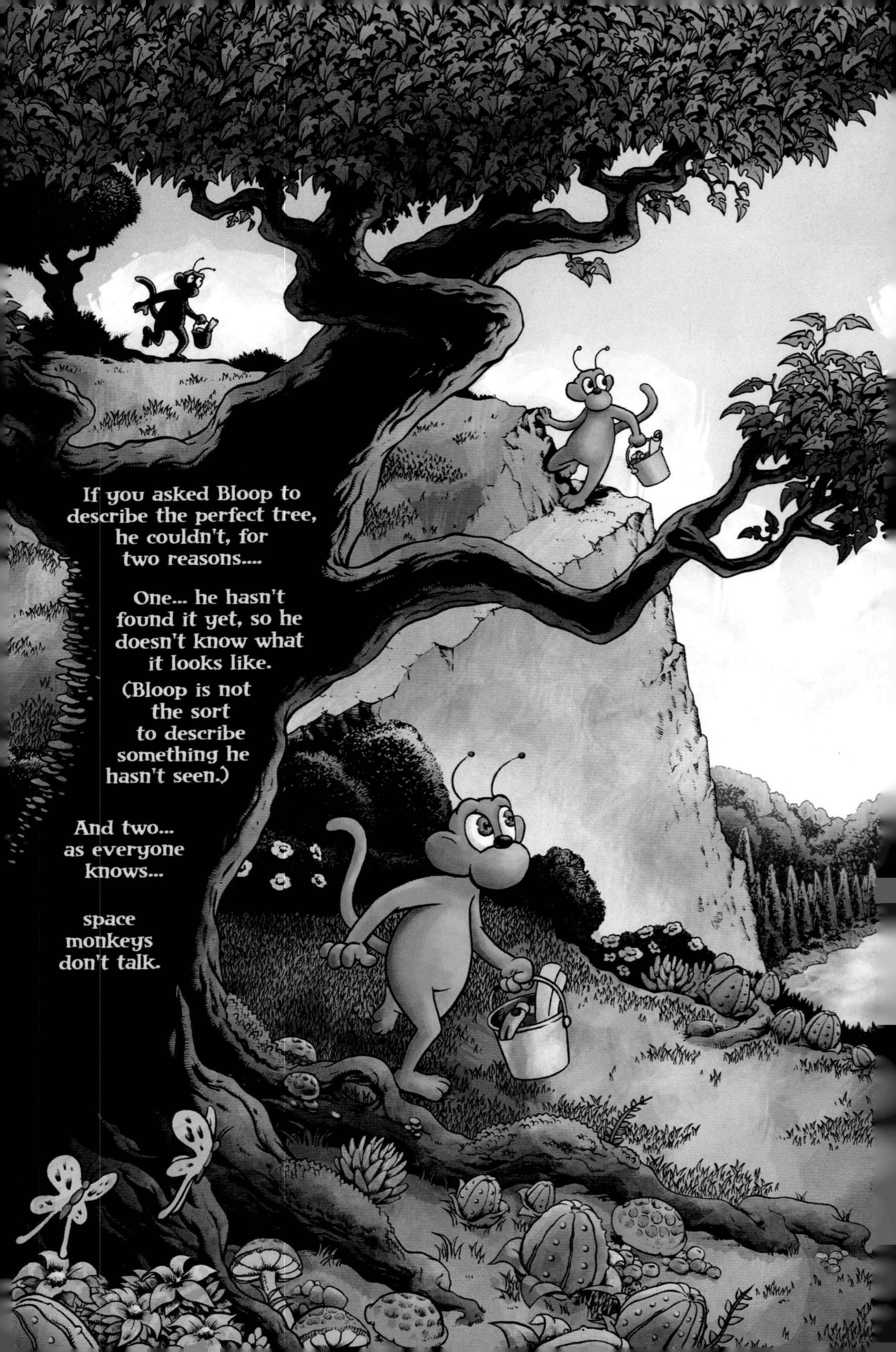
If you asked Bloop to
describe the perfect tree,
he couldn't, for
two reasons....
One... he hasn't
found it yet, so he
doesn't know what
it looks like.
(Bloop is not
the sort
to describe
something he
hasn't seen.)
And two...
as everyone
knows...
space
monkeys
don't talk.

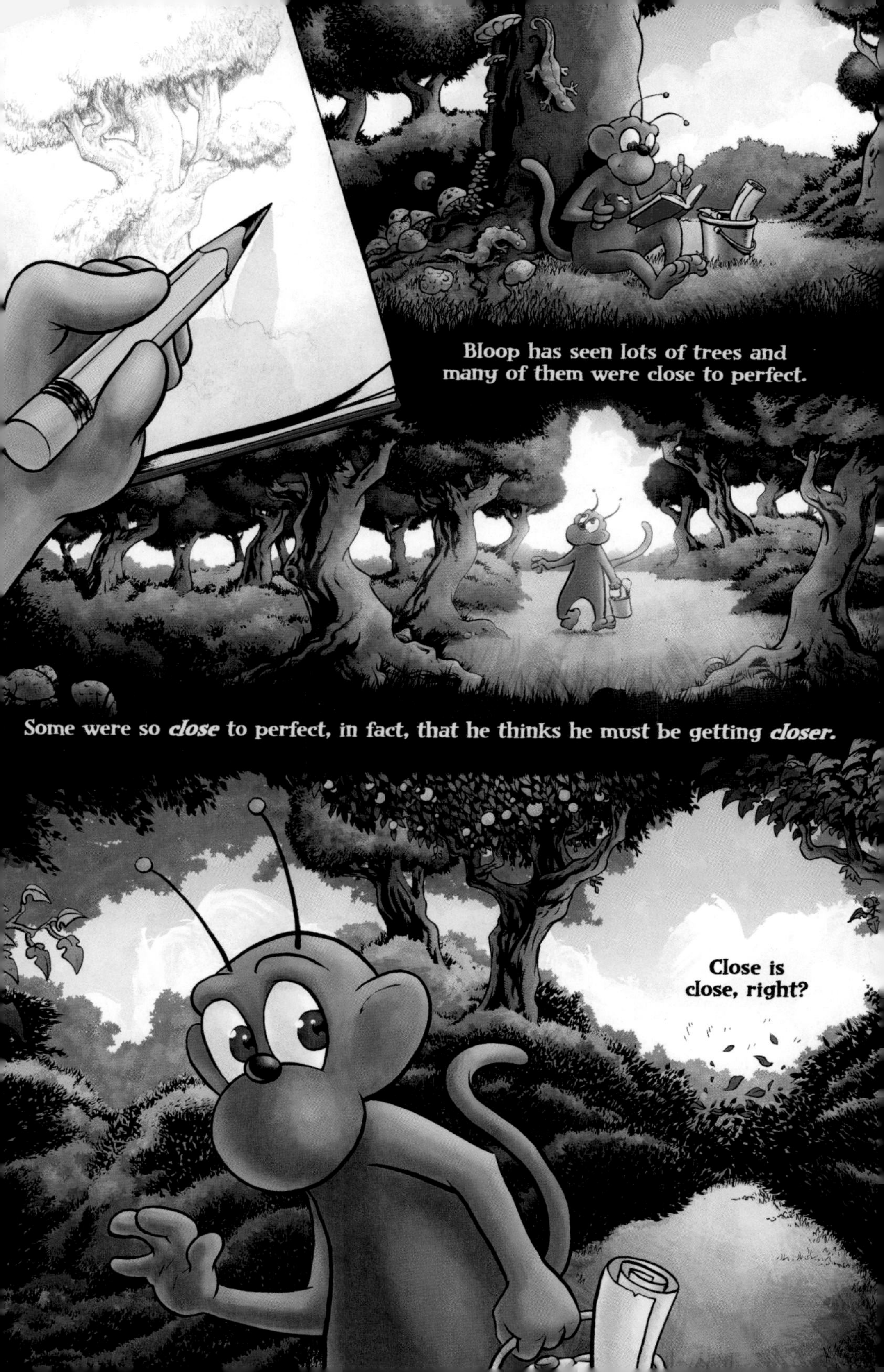
Bloop has seen lots of trees and many of them were close to perfect.
Some were so *close* to perfect, in fact, that he thinks he must be getting *closer.*
Close is close, right?

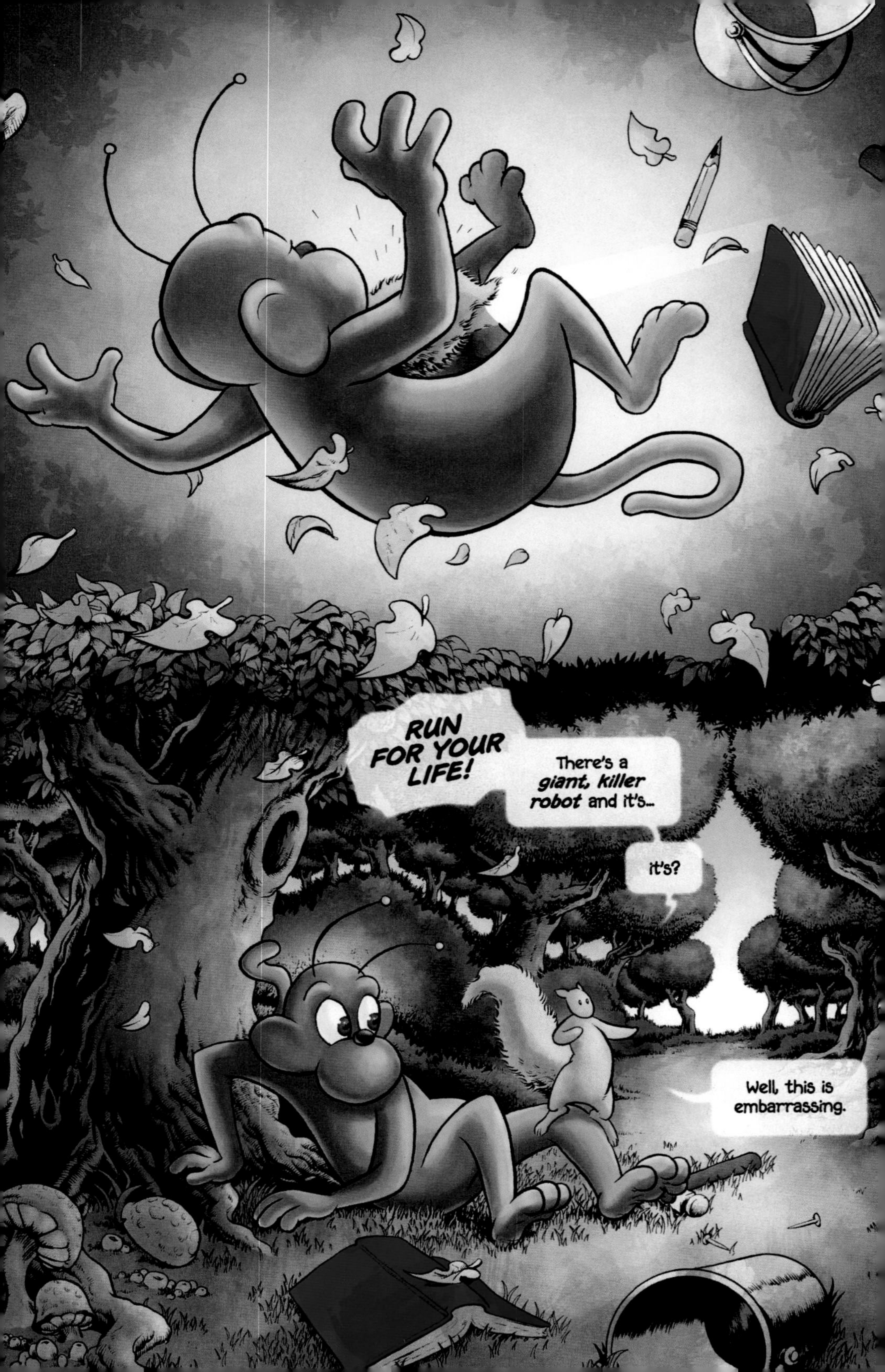

RUN FOR YOUR LIFE!
There's a *giant, killer robot* and it's...
it's?
Well, this is embarrassing.

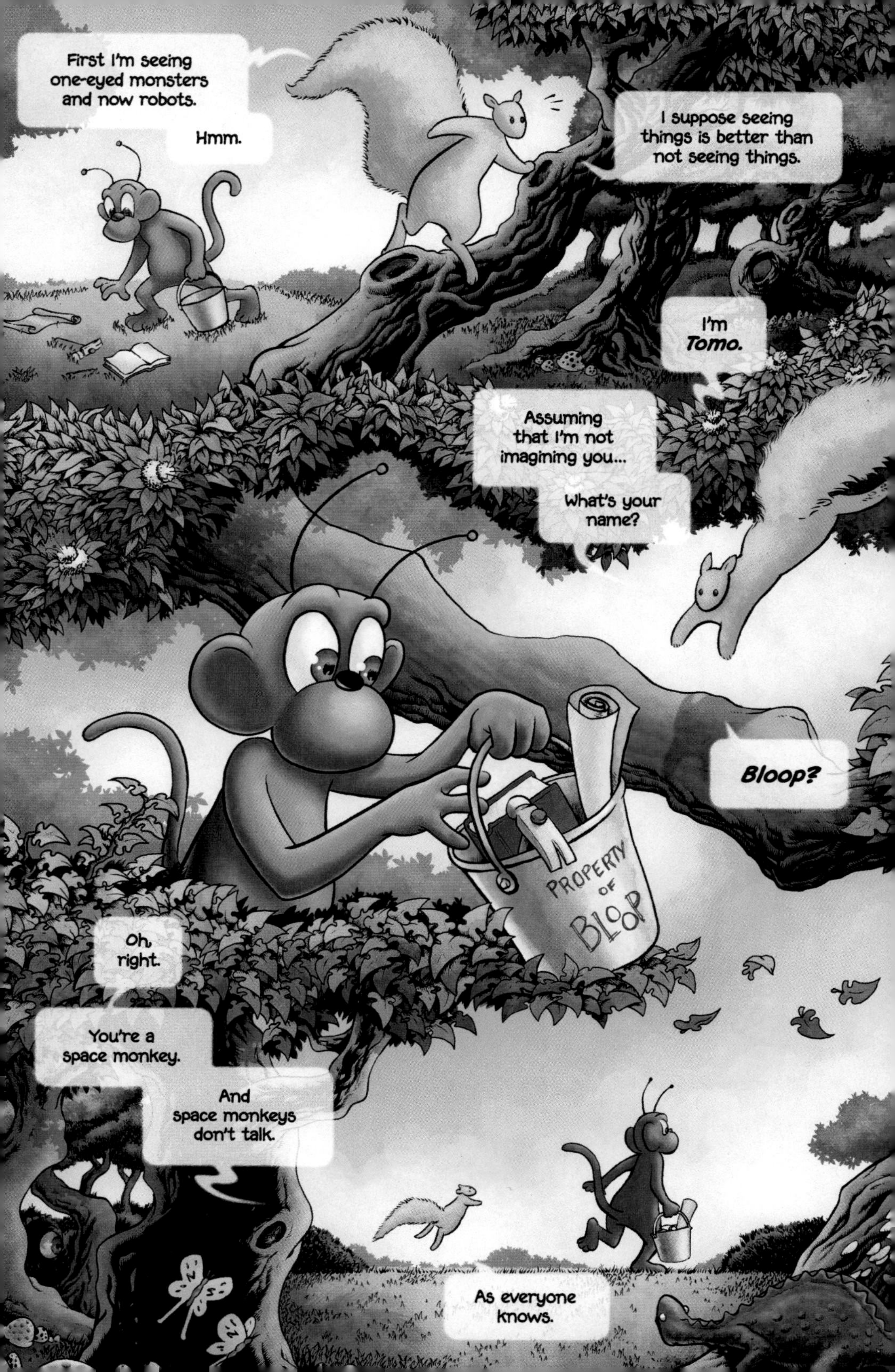
First I'm seeing one-eyed monsters and now robots.
Hmm.
I suppose seeing things is better than not seeing things.
I'm *Tomo.*
Assuming that I'm not imagining you...
What's your name?
Bloop?
PROPERTY OF BLOOP
Oh, right.
You're a space monkey.
And space monkeys don't talk.
As everyone knows.

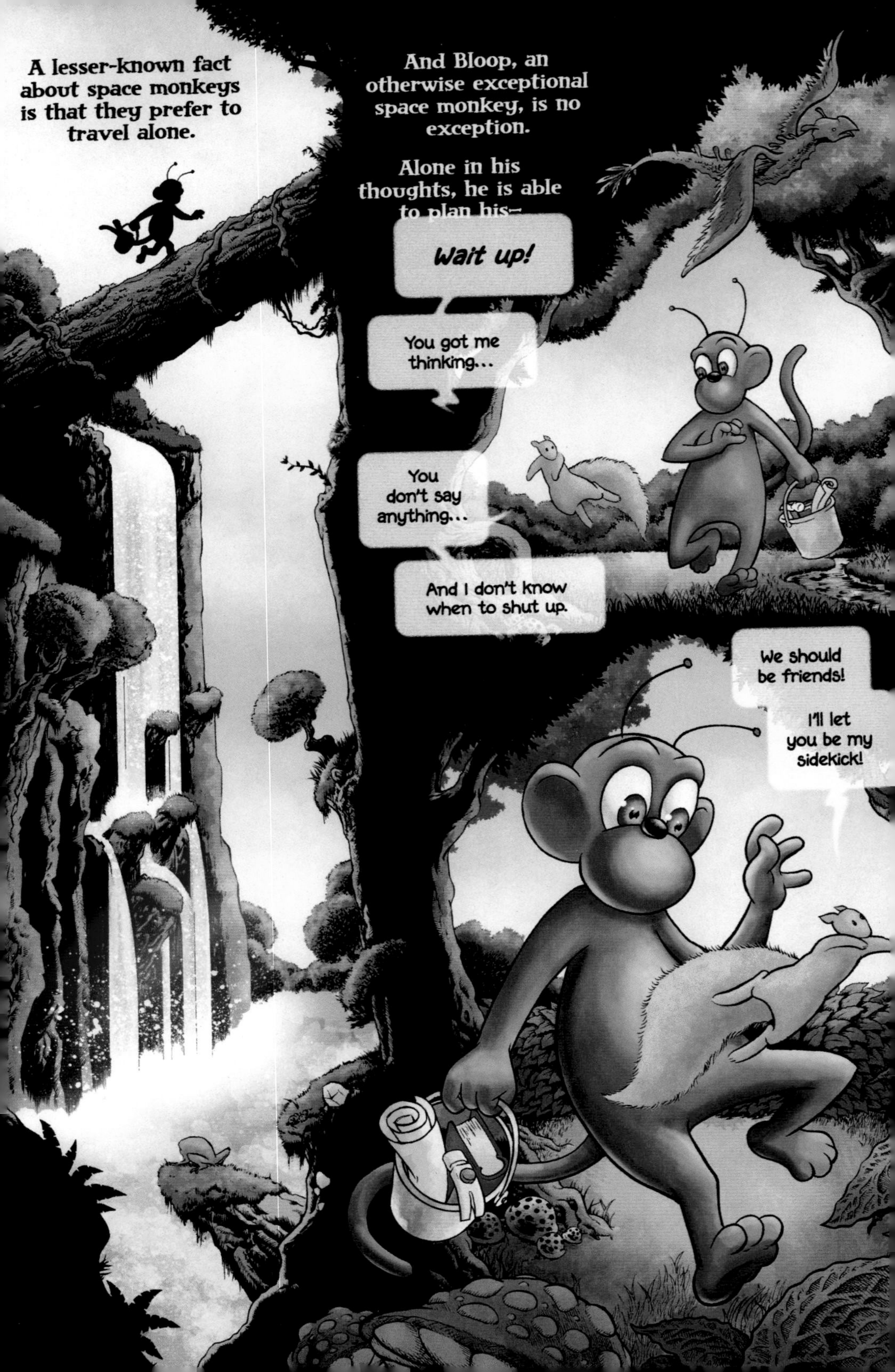
A lesser-known fact about space monkeys is that they prefer to travel alone.
And Bloop, an otherwise exceptional space monkey, is no exception.
Alone in his thoughts, he is able to plan his—
Wait up!
You got me thinking...
You don't say anything...
And I don't know when to shut up.
We should be friends!
I'll let you be my sidekick!

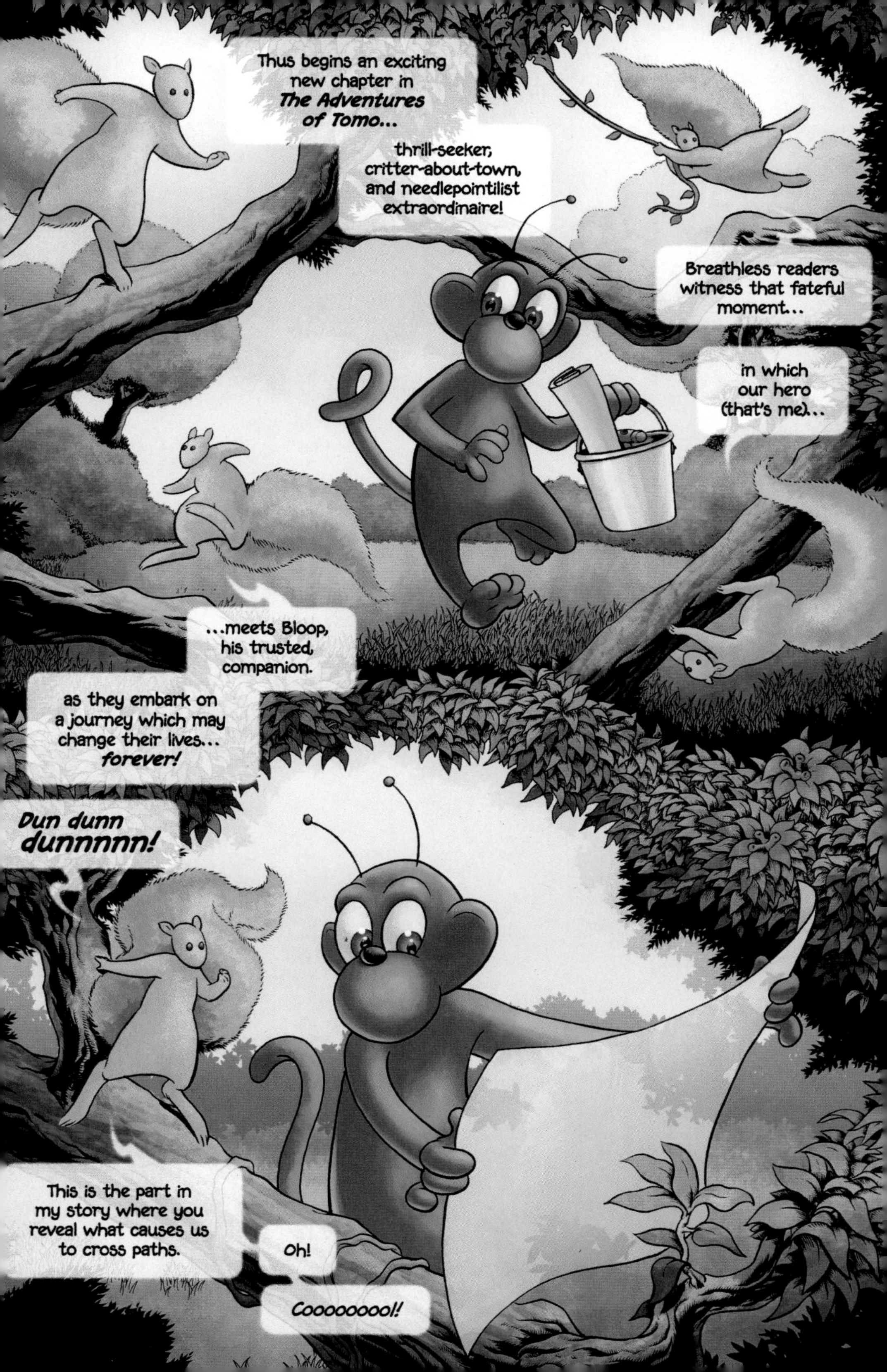
Thus begins an exciting new chapter in *The Adventures of Tomo...*
thrill-seeker, critter-about-town, and needlepointilist extraordinaire!
Breathless readers witness that fateful moment...
in which our hero (that's me)...
...meets Bloop, his trusted companion.
as they embark on a journey which may change their lives... *forever!*
Dun dunn dunnnnn!
This is the part in my story where you reveal what causes us to cross paths.
Oh!
Cooooooool!

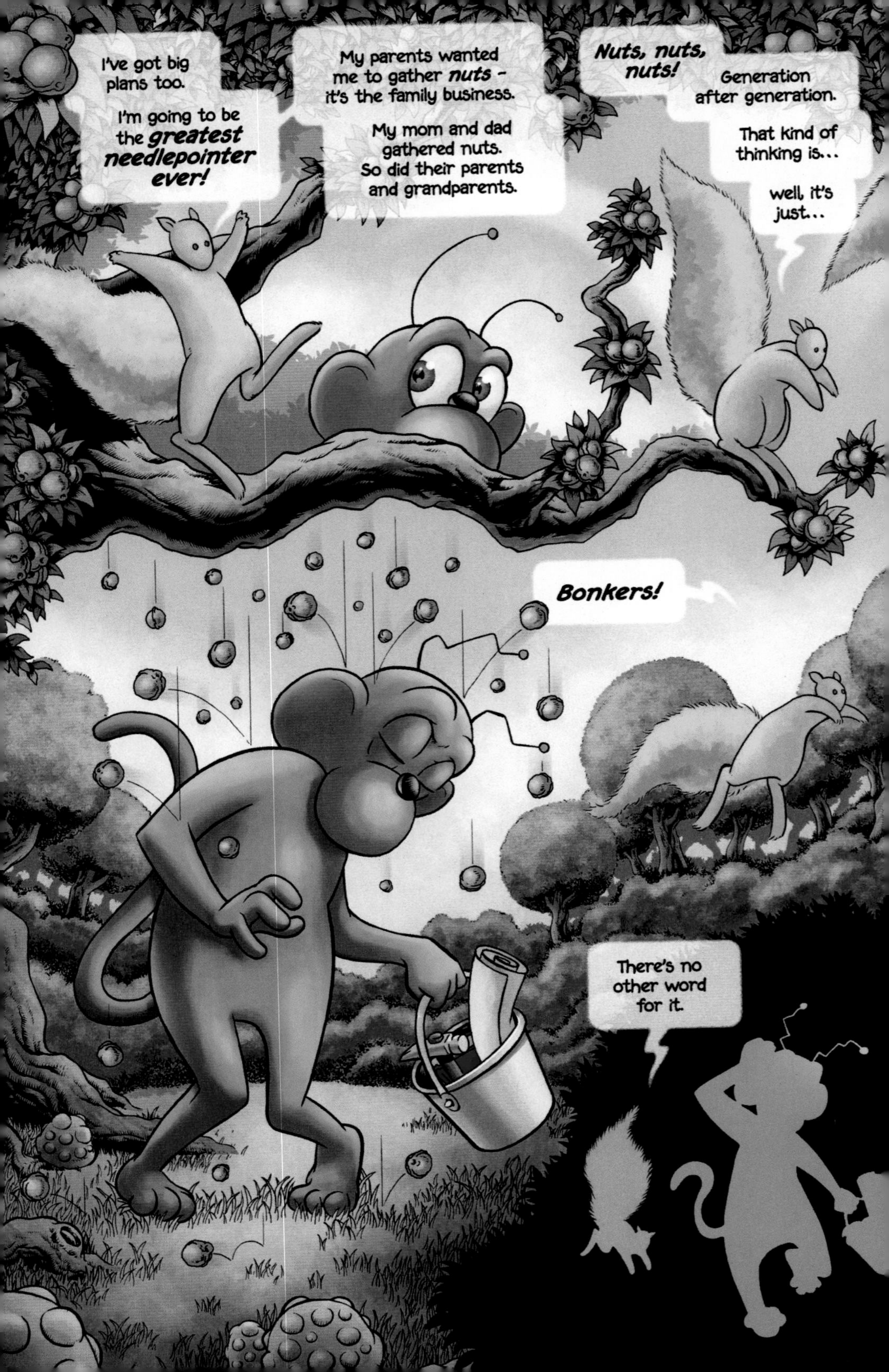
I've got big plans too.
I'm going to be the *greatest needlepointer ever!*
My parents wanted me to gather *nuts* - it's the family business.
My mom and dad gathered nuts. So did their parents and grandparents.
Nuts, nuts, nuts!
Generation after generation.
That kind of thinking is...
well, it's just...
Bonkers!
There's no other word for it.

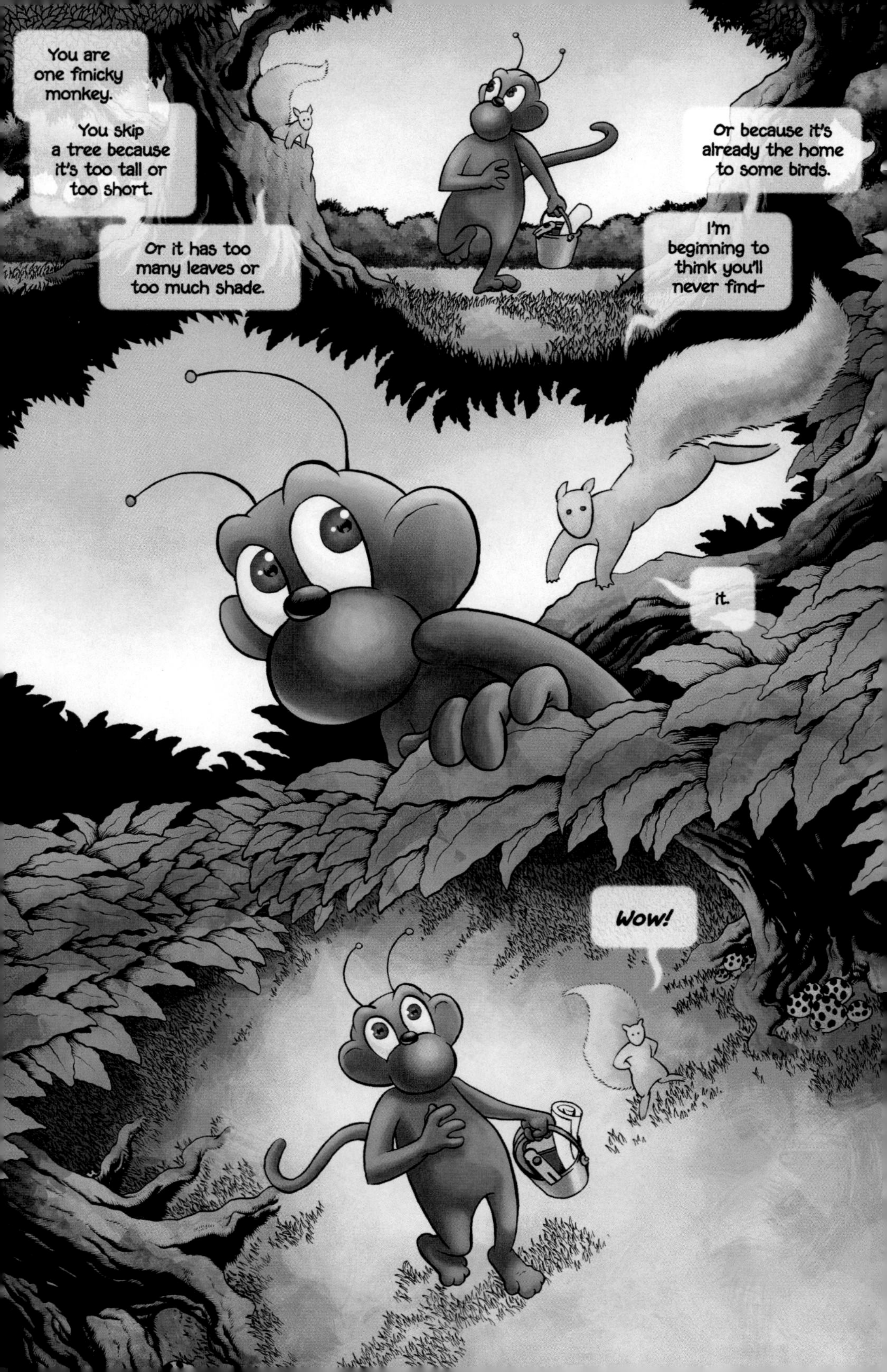
You are one finicky monkey.
You skip a tree because it's too tall or too short.
Or it has too many leaves or too much shade.
Or because it's already the home to some birds.
I'm beginning to think you'll never find-
it.
WOW!

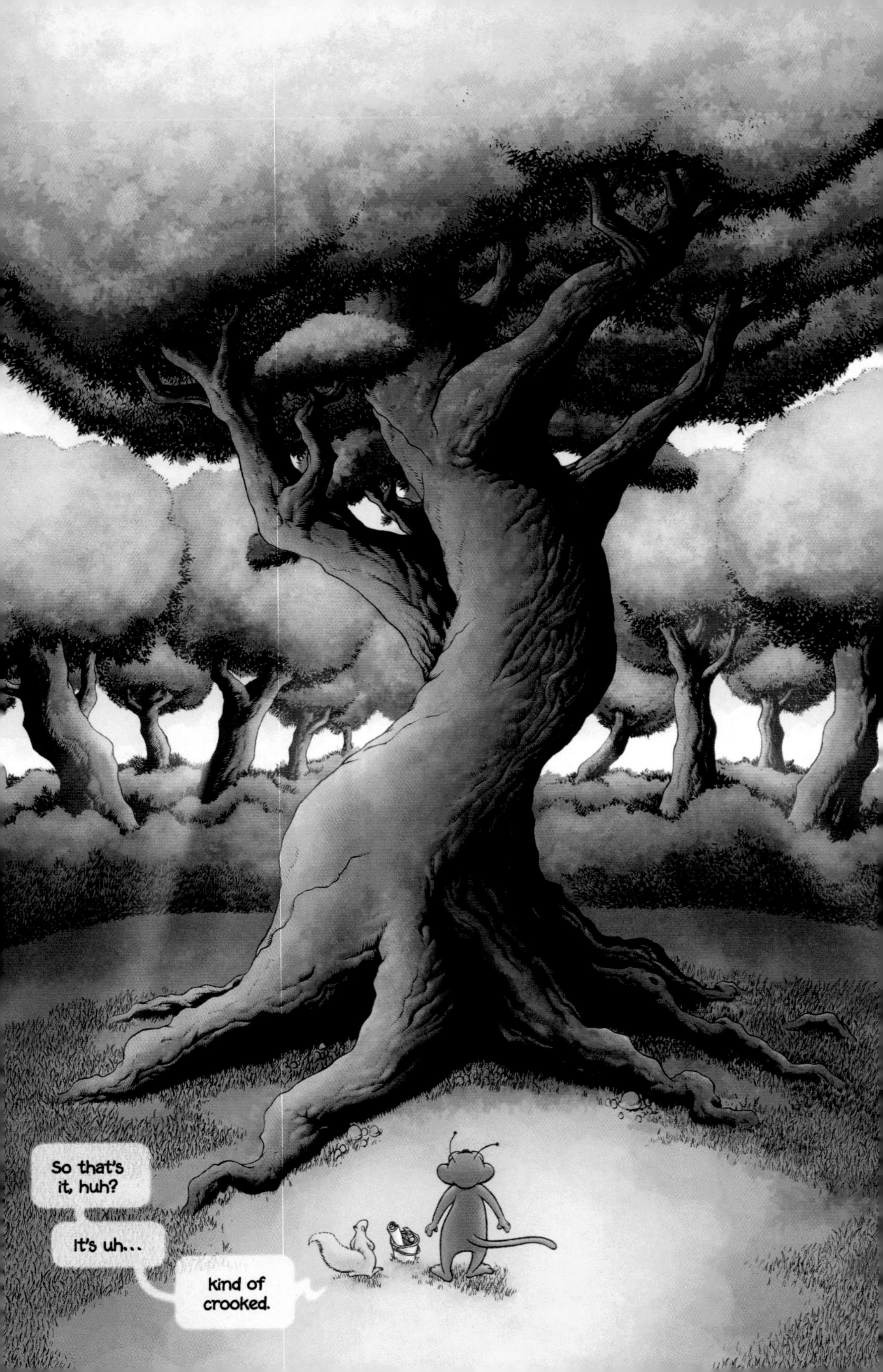
So that's it, huh?
It's uh...
kind of crooked.

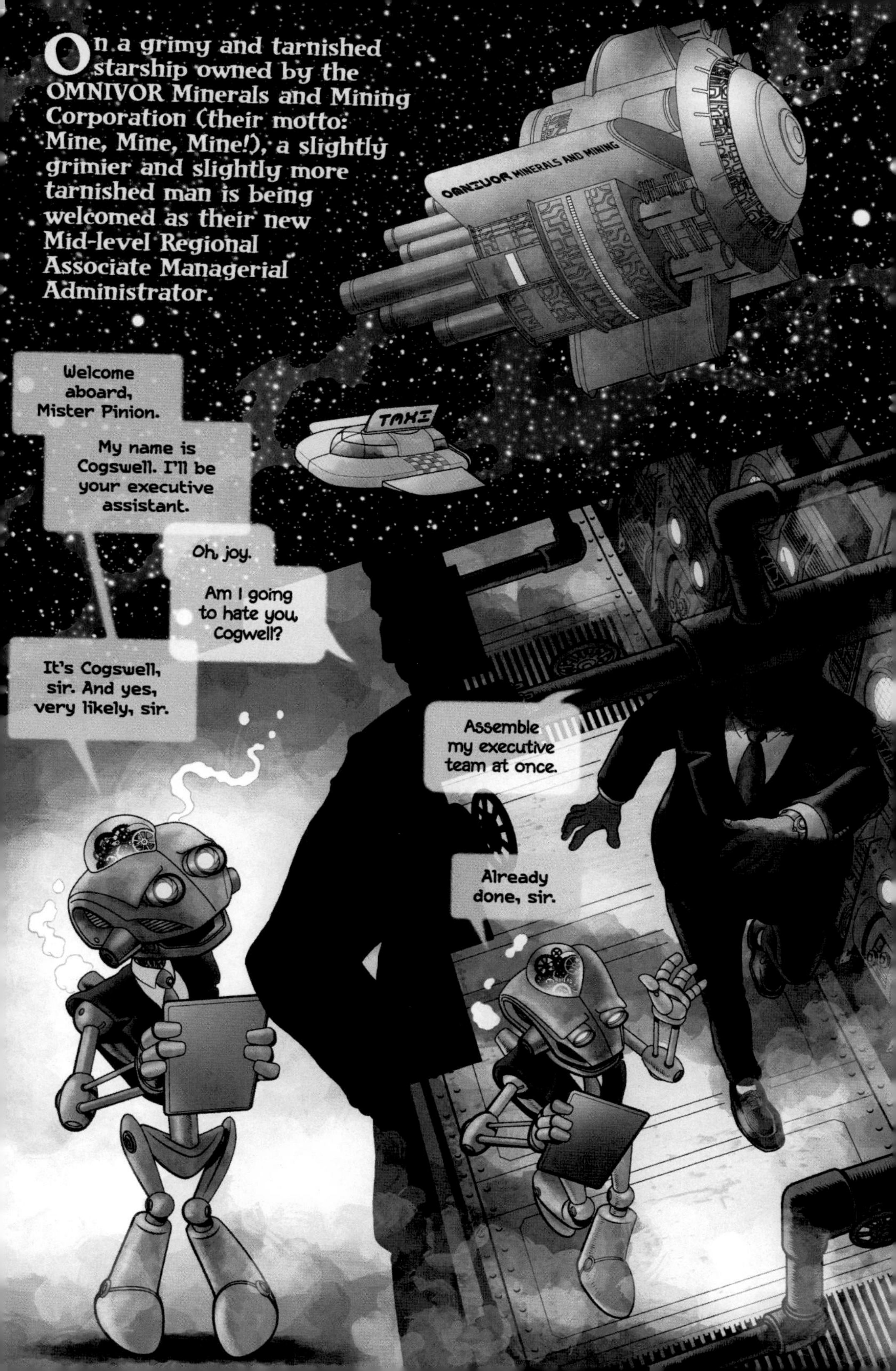
On a grimy and tarnished starship owned by the OMNIVOR Minerals and Mining Corporation (their motto: Mine, Mine, Mine!), a slightly grimier and slightly more tarnished man is being welcomed as their new Mid-level Regional Associate Managerial Administrator.
OMNIVOR MINERALS AND MINING
TAXI
Welcome aboard, Mister Pinion.
My name is Cogswell. I'll be your executive assistant.
Oh, joy.
Am I going to hate you, Cogwell?
It's Cogswell, sir. And yes, very likely, sir.
Assemble my executive team at once.
Already done, sir.

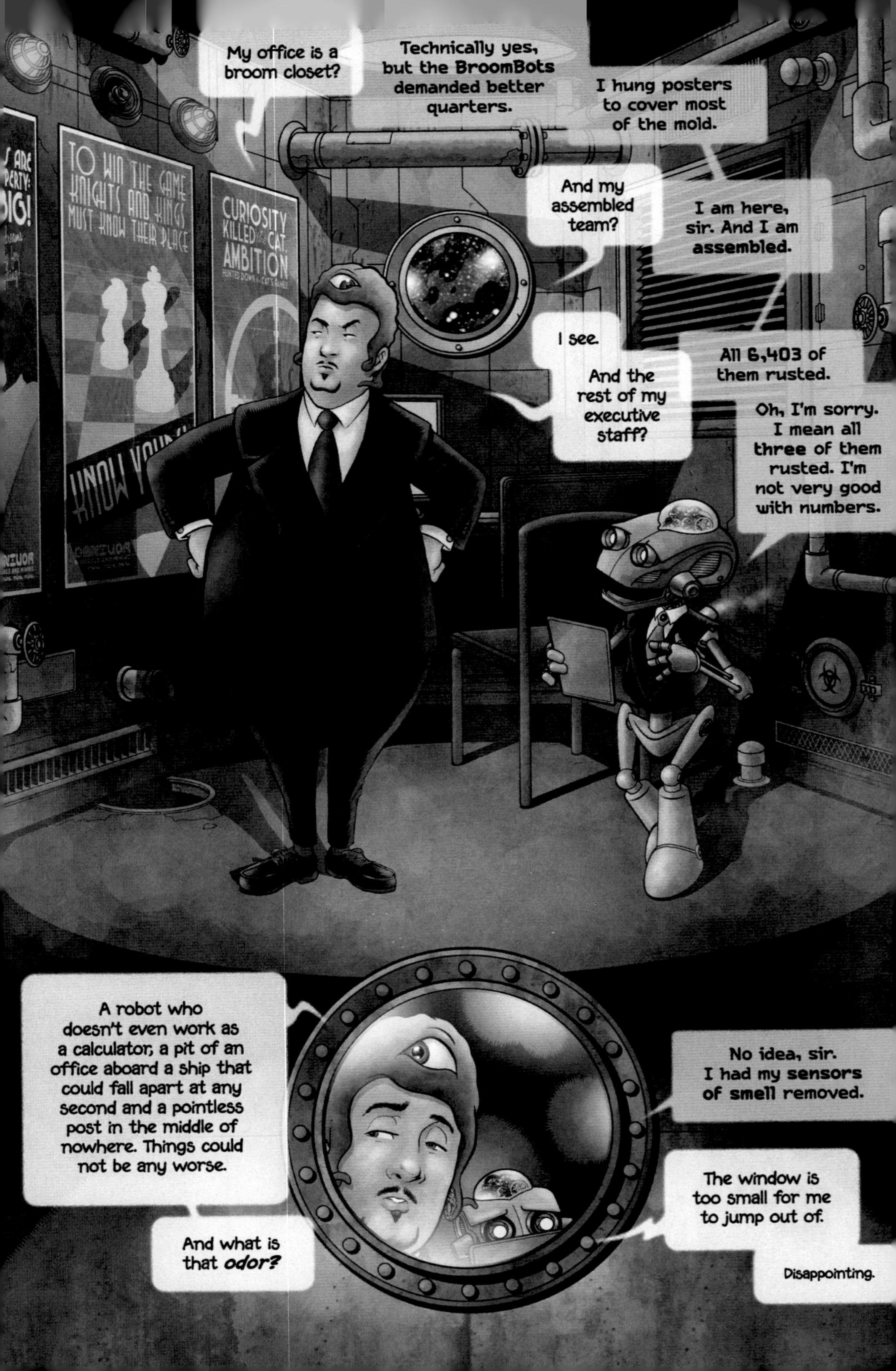
My office is a broom closet?
Technically yes, but the BroomBots demanded better quarters.
I hung posters to cover most of the mold.
TO WIN THE GAME KNIGHTS AND KINGS MUST KNOW THEIR PLACE
CURIOSITY KILLED THE CAT. AMBITION
KNOW YOUR
And my assembled team?
I am here, sir. And I am assembled.
I see.
And the rest of my executive staff?
All 6,403 of them rusted.
Oh, I'm sorry. I mean all three of them rusted. I'm not very good with numbers.
A robot who doesn't even work as a calculator, a pit of an office aboard a ship that could fall apart at any second and a pointless post in the middle of nowhere. Things could not be any worse.
And what is that *odor?*
No idea, sir. I had my sensors of smell removed.
The window is too small for me to jump out of.
Disappointing.

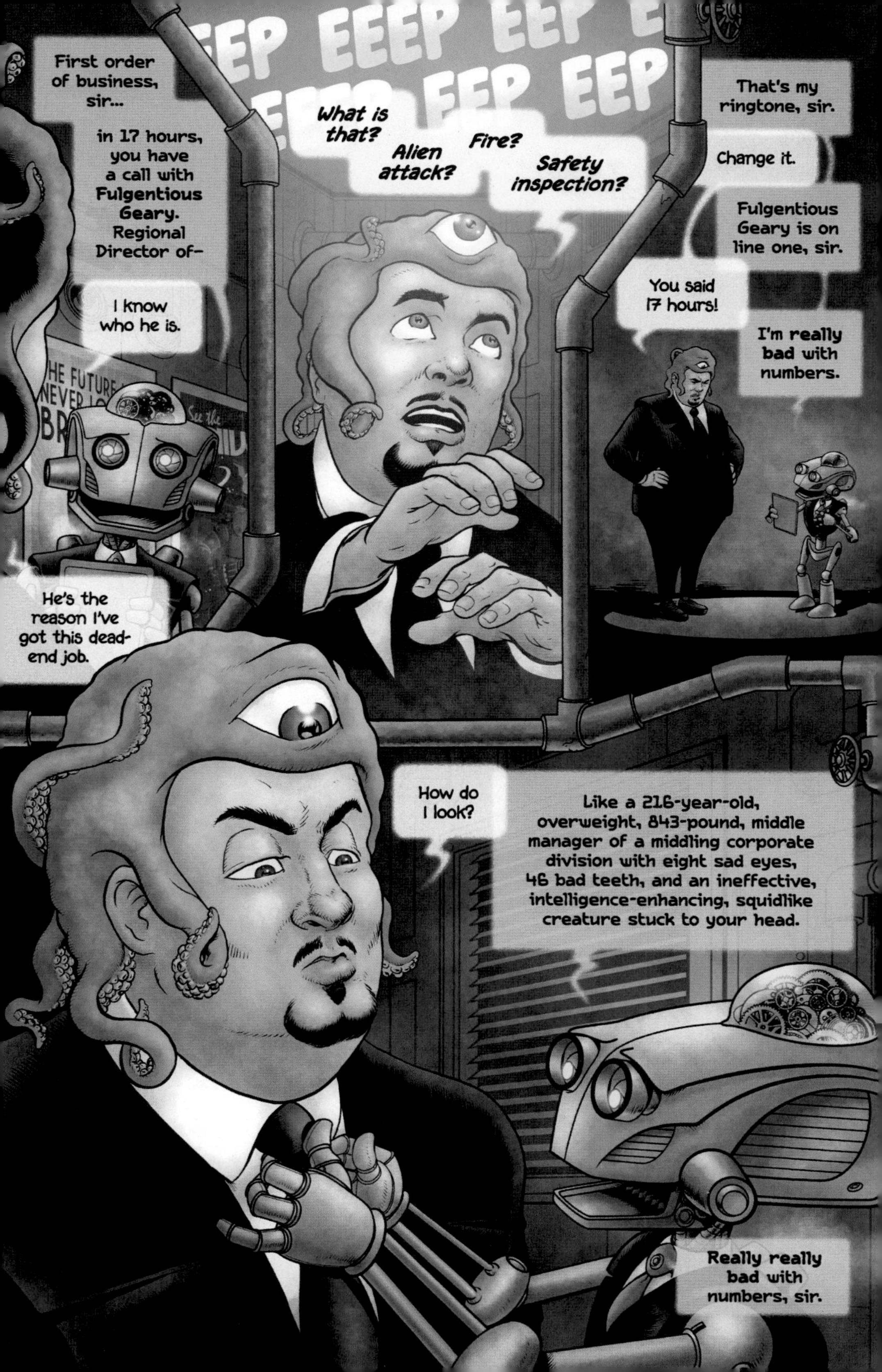

EEEP EEEP EEEP EEEP EEEP EEEP
First order of business, sir...
in 17 hours, you have a call with Fulgentious Geary. Regional Director of–
I know who he is.
He's the reason I've got this dead-end job.
What is that?
Alien attack?
Fire?
Safety inspection?
That's my ringtone, sir.
Change it.
Fulgentious Geary is on line one, sir.
You said 17 hours!
I'm really bad with numbers.
How do I look?
Like a 216-year-old, overweight, 843-pound, middle manager of a middling corporate division with eight sad eyes, 46 bad teeth, and an ineffective, intelligence-enhancing, squidlike creature stuck to your head.
Really really bad with numbers, sir.

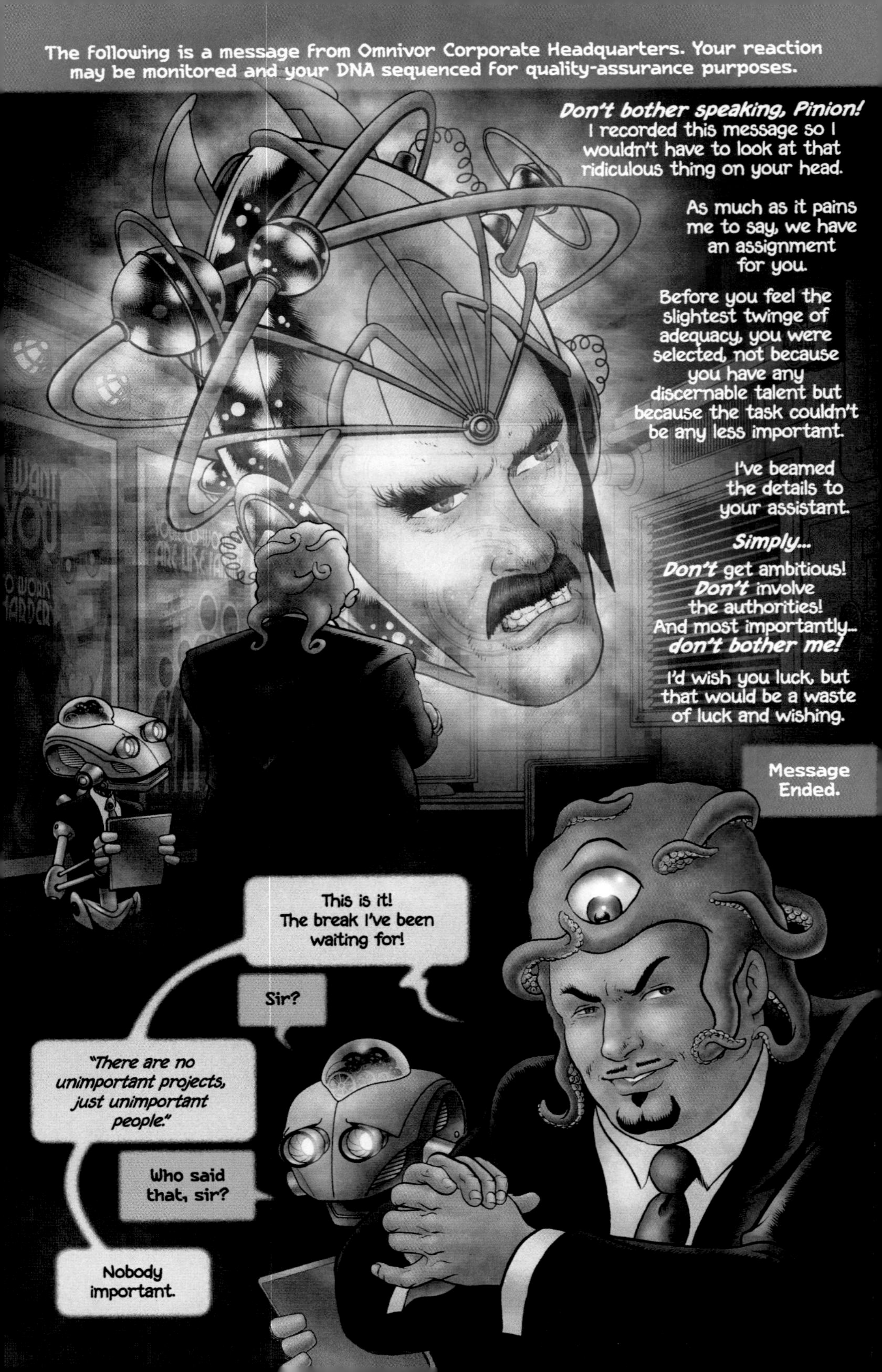
The following is a message from Omnivor Corporate Headquarters. Your reaction may be monitored and your DNA sequenced for quality-assurance purposes.
Don't bother speaking, Pinion! I recorded this message so I wouldn't have to look at that ridiculous thing on your head.
As much as it pains me to say, we have an assignment for you.
Before you feel the slightest twinge of adequacy, you were selected, not because you have any discernable talent but because the task couldn't be any less important.
I've beamed the details to your assistant.
Simply...
Don't get ambitious! Don't involve the authorities! And most importantly... don't bother me!
I'd wish you luck, but that would be a waste of luck and wishing.
Message Ended.
This is it! The break I've been waiting for!
Sir?
"There are no unimportant projects, just unimportant people."
Who said that, sir?
Nobody important.

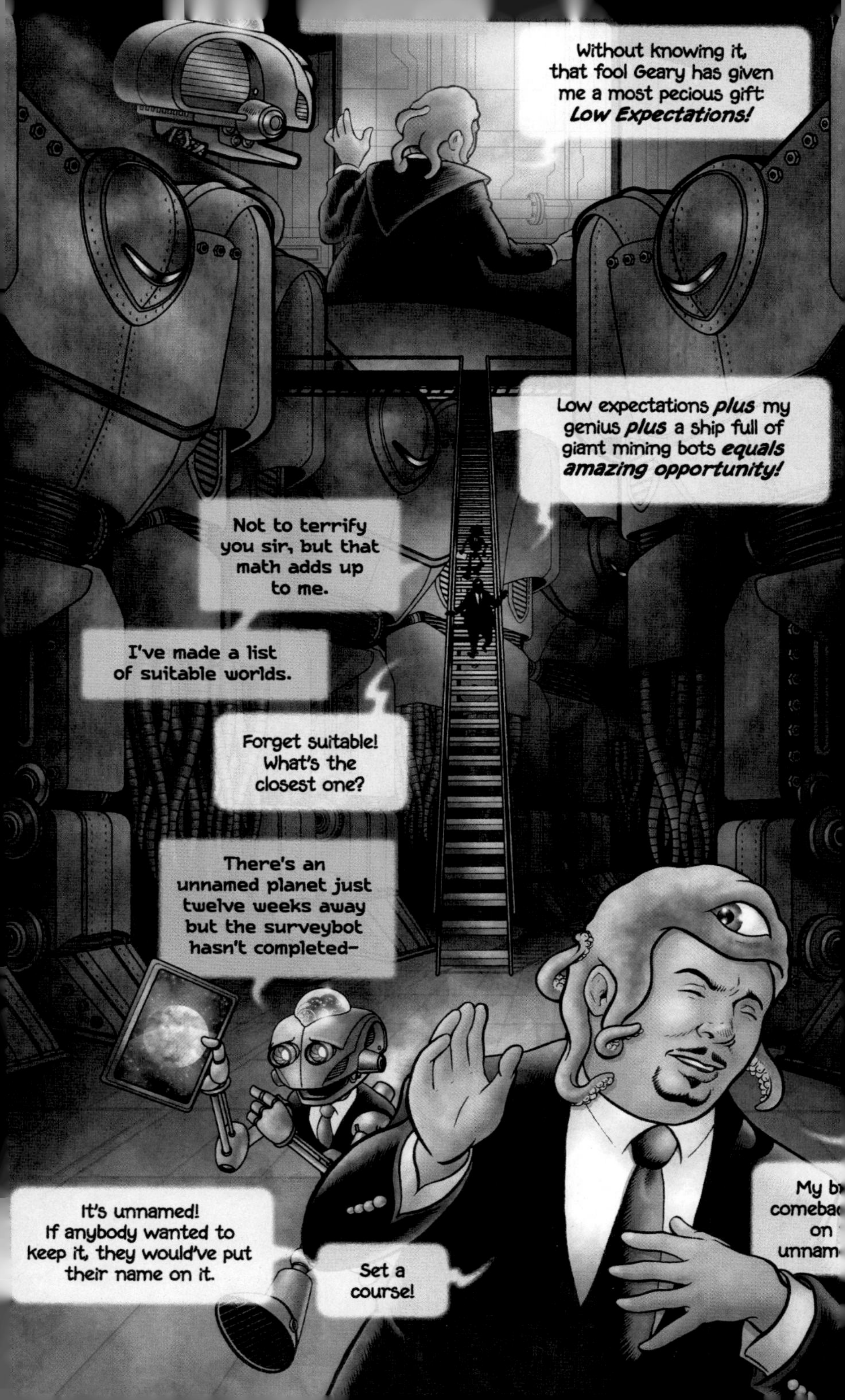
Without knowing it, that fool Geary has given me a most pecious gift: ***Low Expectations!***
Low expectations ***plus*** my genius ***plus*** a ship full of giant mining bots ***equals amazing opportunity!***
Not to terrify you sir, but that math adds up to me.
I've made a list of suitable worlds.
Forget suitable! What's the closest one?
There's an unnamed planet just twelve weeks away but the surveybot hasn't completed–
It's unnamed! If anybody wanted to keep it, they would've put their name on it.
Set a course!

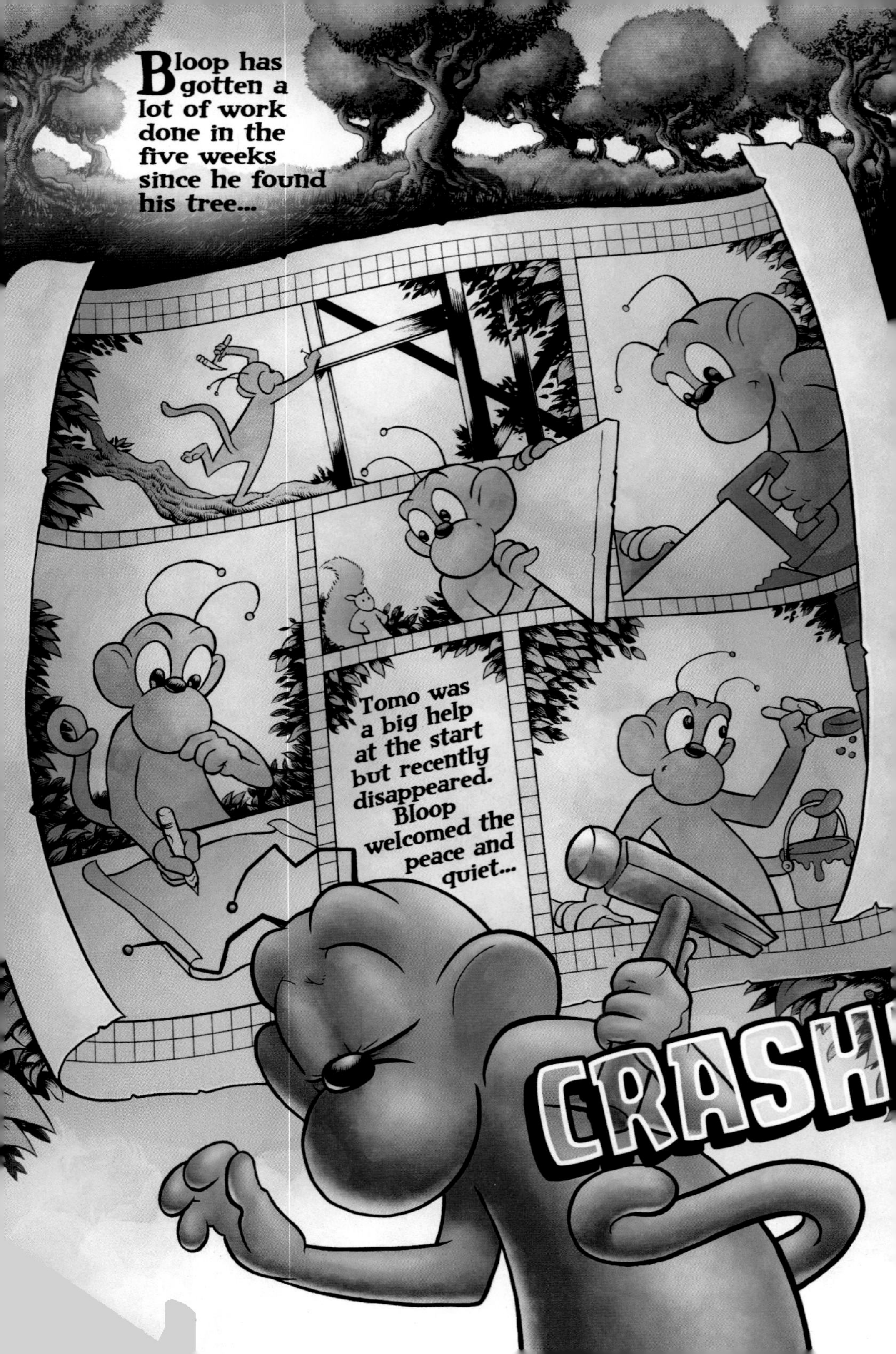

Bloop has gotten a lot of work done in the five weeks since he found his tree...
Tomo was a big help at the start but recently disappeared. Bloop welcomed the peace and quiet...
CRASH

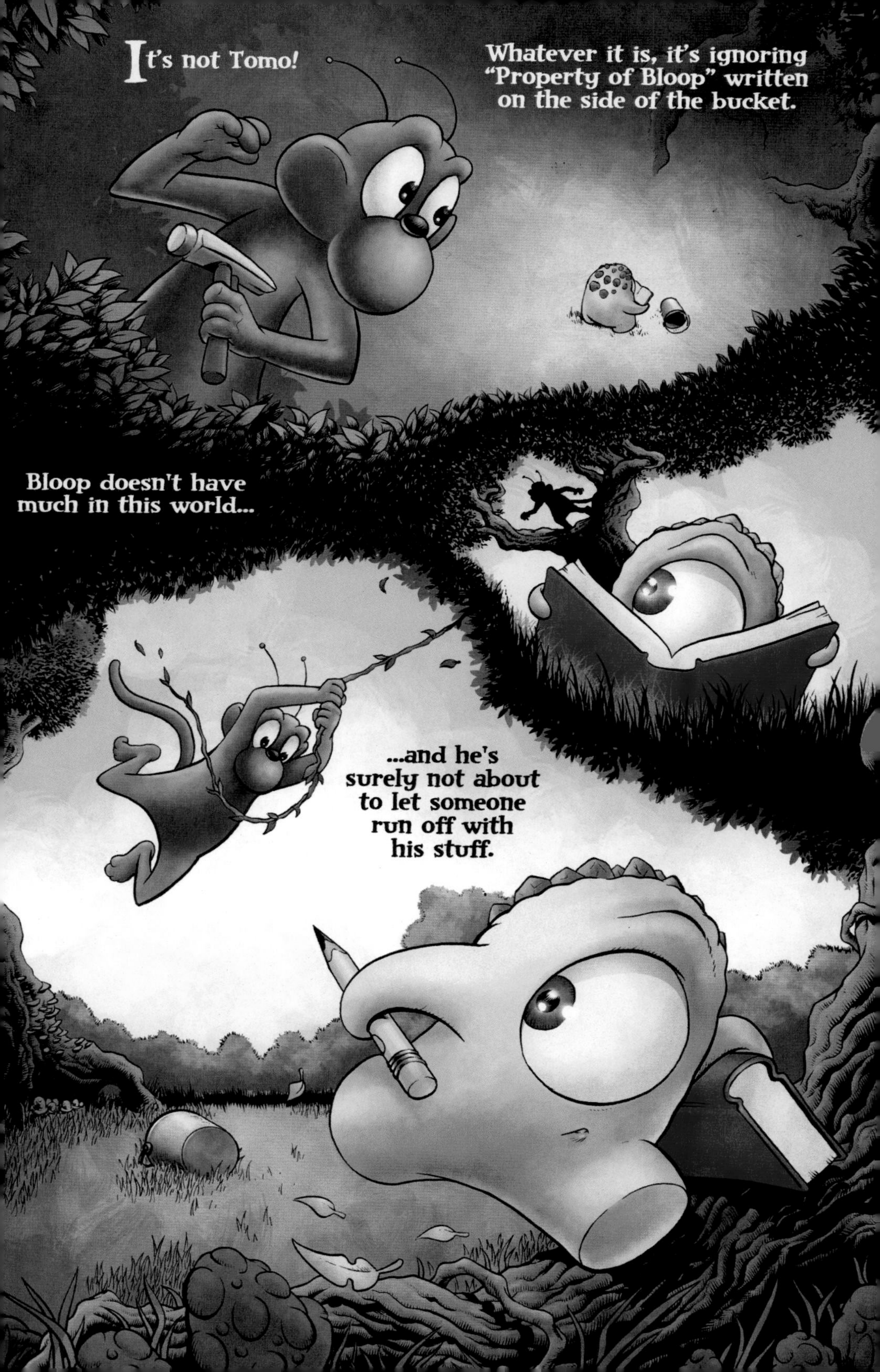
It's not Tomo!
Whatever it is, it's ignoring "Property of Bloop" written on the side of the bucket.
Bloop doesn't have much in this world...
...and he's surely not about to let someone run off with his stuff.

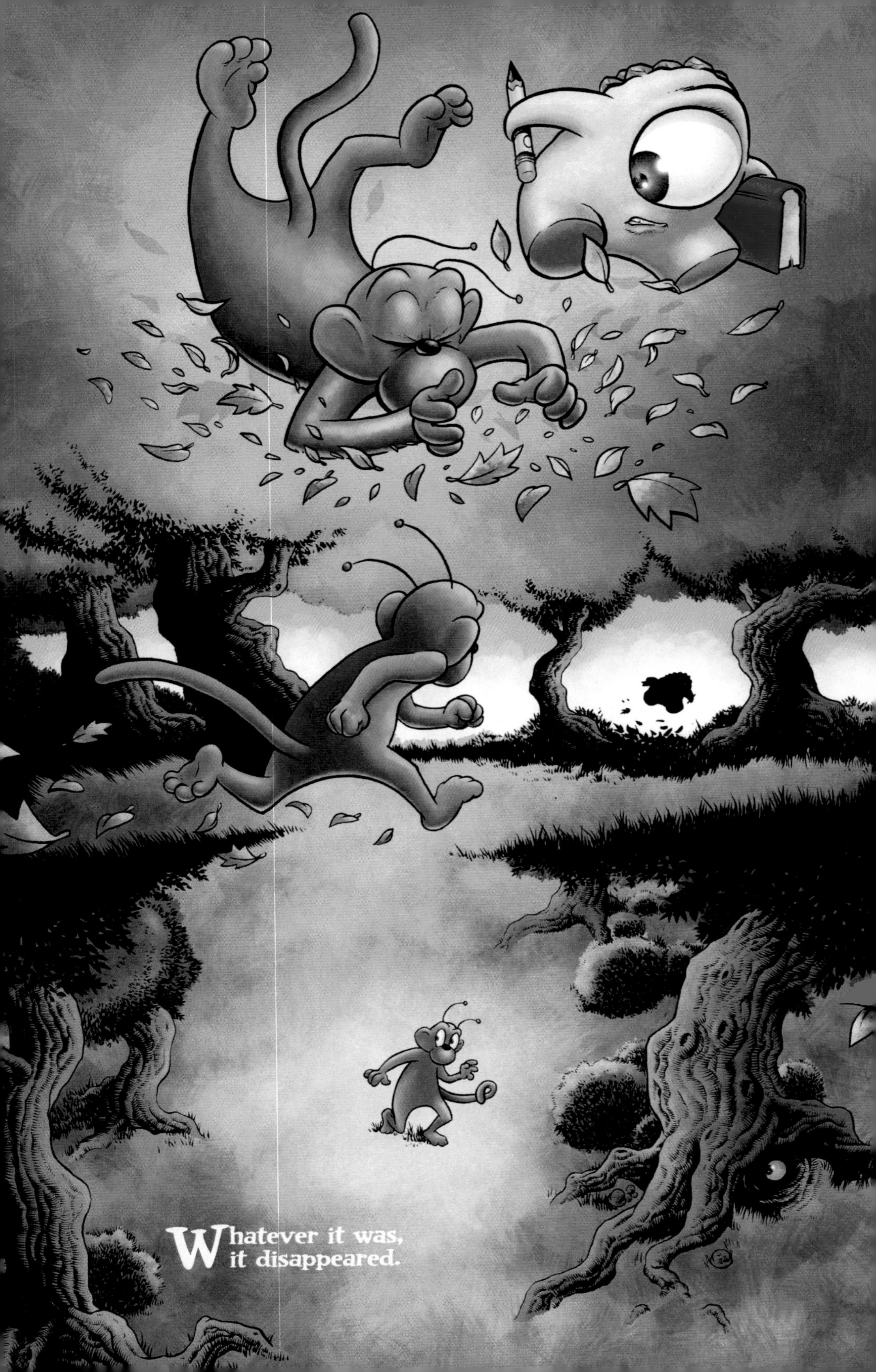
Whatever it was, it disappeared.

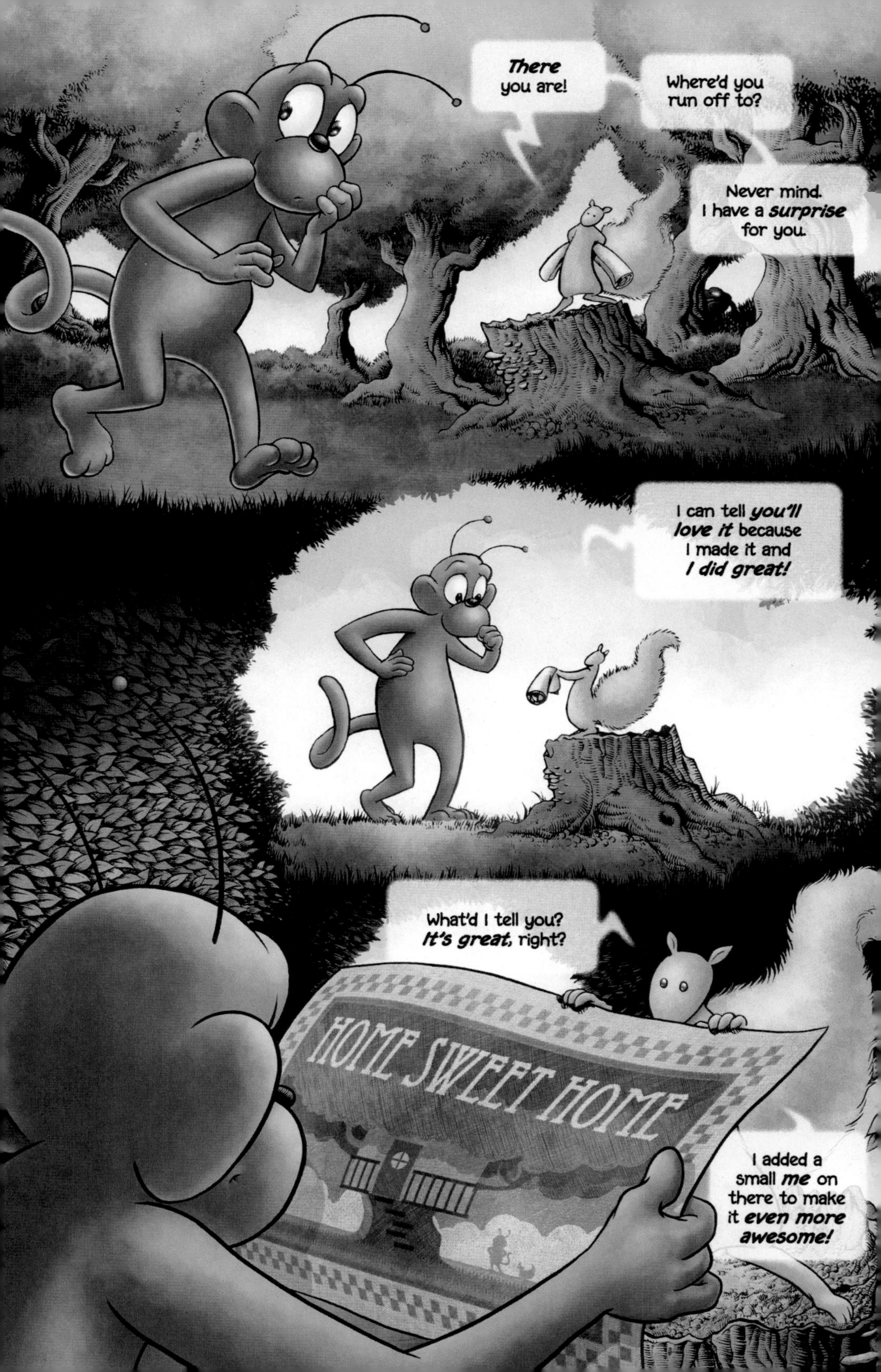
There you are!
Where'd you run off to?
Never mind. I have a surprise for you.
I can tell you'll love it because I made it and I did great!
What'd I tell you? It's great, right?
HOME SWEET HOME
I added a small me on there to make it even more awesome!

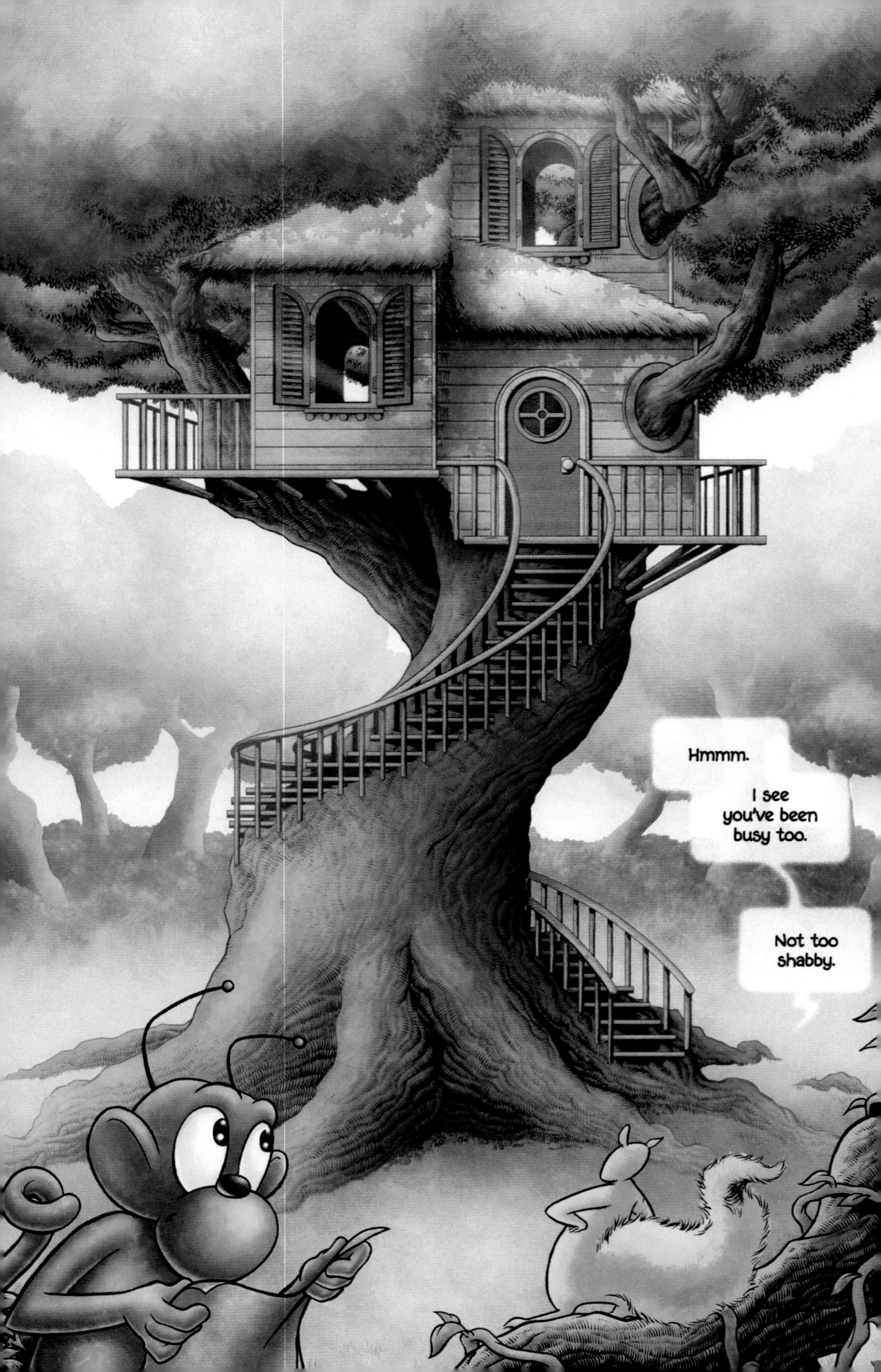
Hmmm.
I see you've been busy too.
Not too shabby.

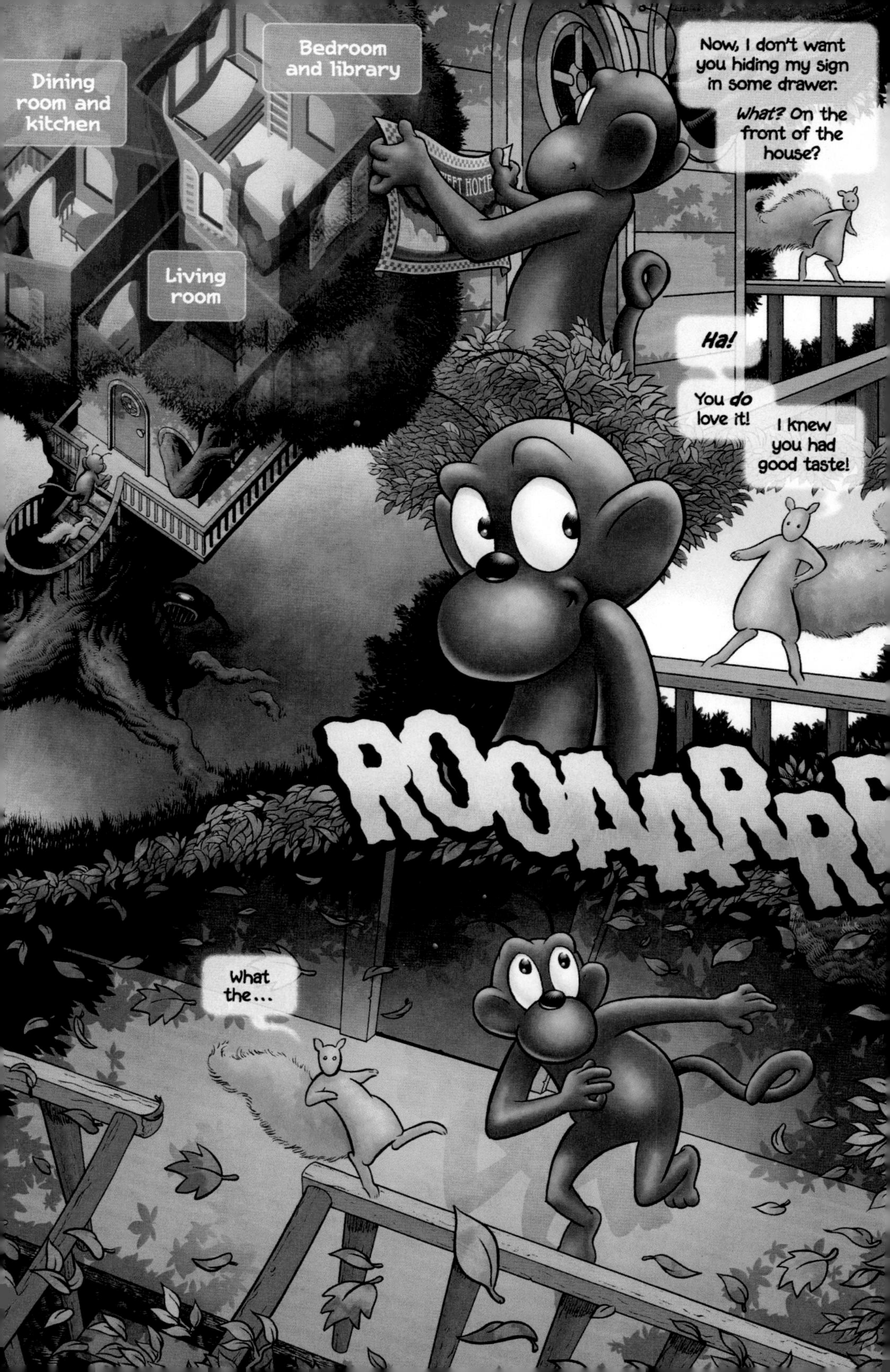
Dining room and kitchen
Bedroom and library
Living room
Now, I don't want you hiding my sign in some drawer.
What? On the front of the house?
Ha!
You do love it!
I knew you had good taste!
ROOARRR
What the...

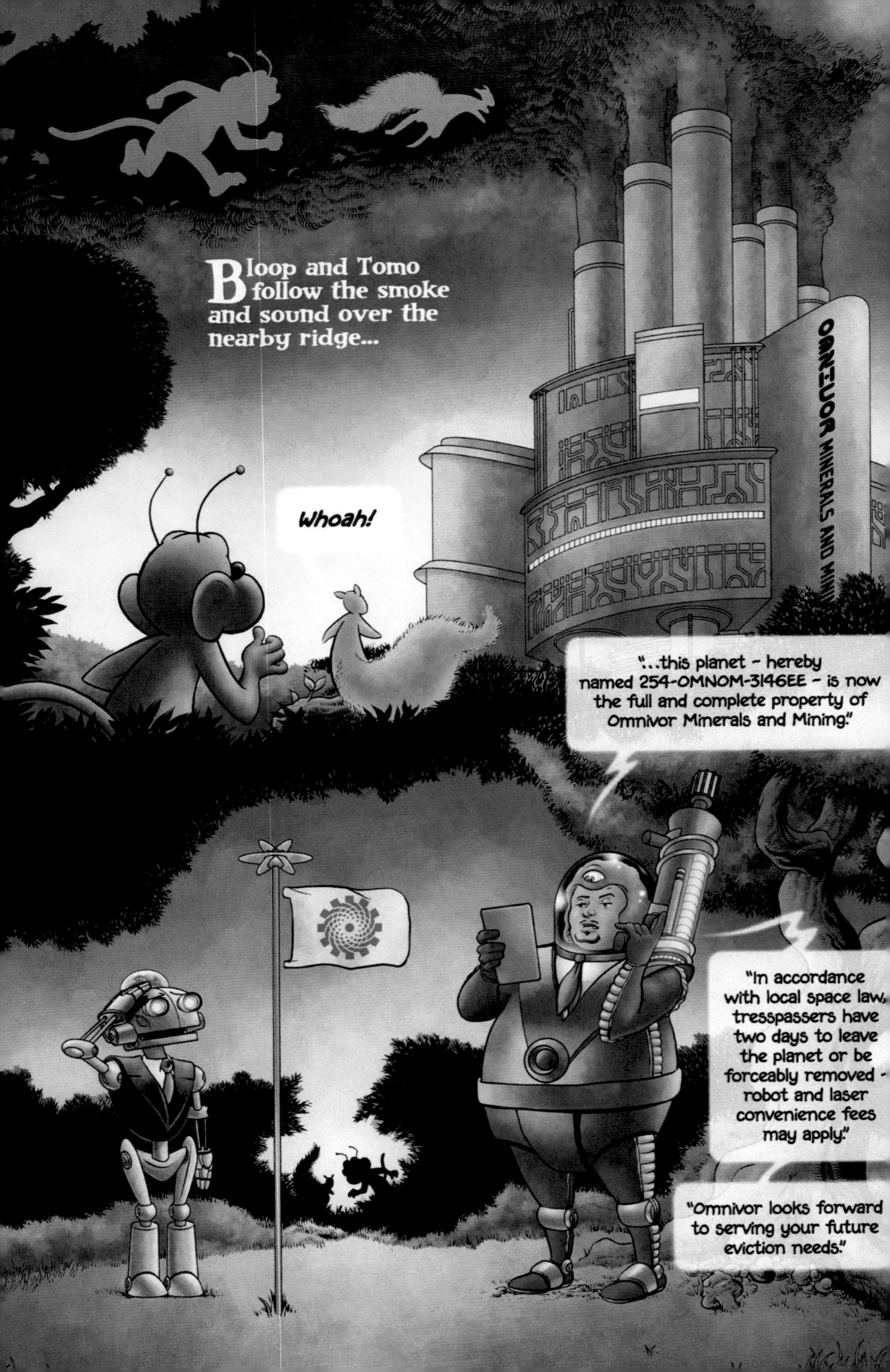
Bloop and Tomo follow the smoke and sound over the nearby ridge...
OMNIVOR MINERALS AND MINI
Whoah!
"...this planet - hereby named 254-OMNOM-3146EE - is now the full and complete property of Omnivor Minerals and Mining."
"In accordance with local space law, tresspassers have two days to leave the planet or be forceably removed - robot and laser convenience fees may apply."
"Omnivor looks forward to serving your future eviction needs."

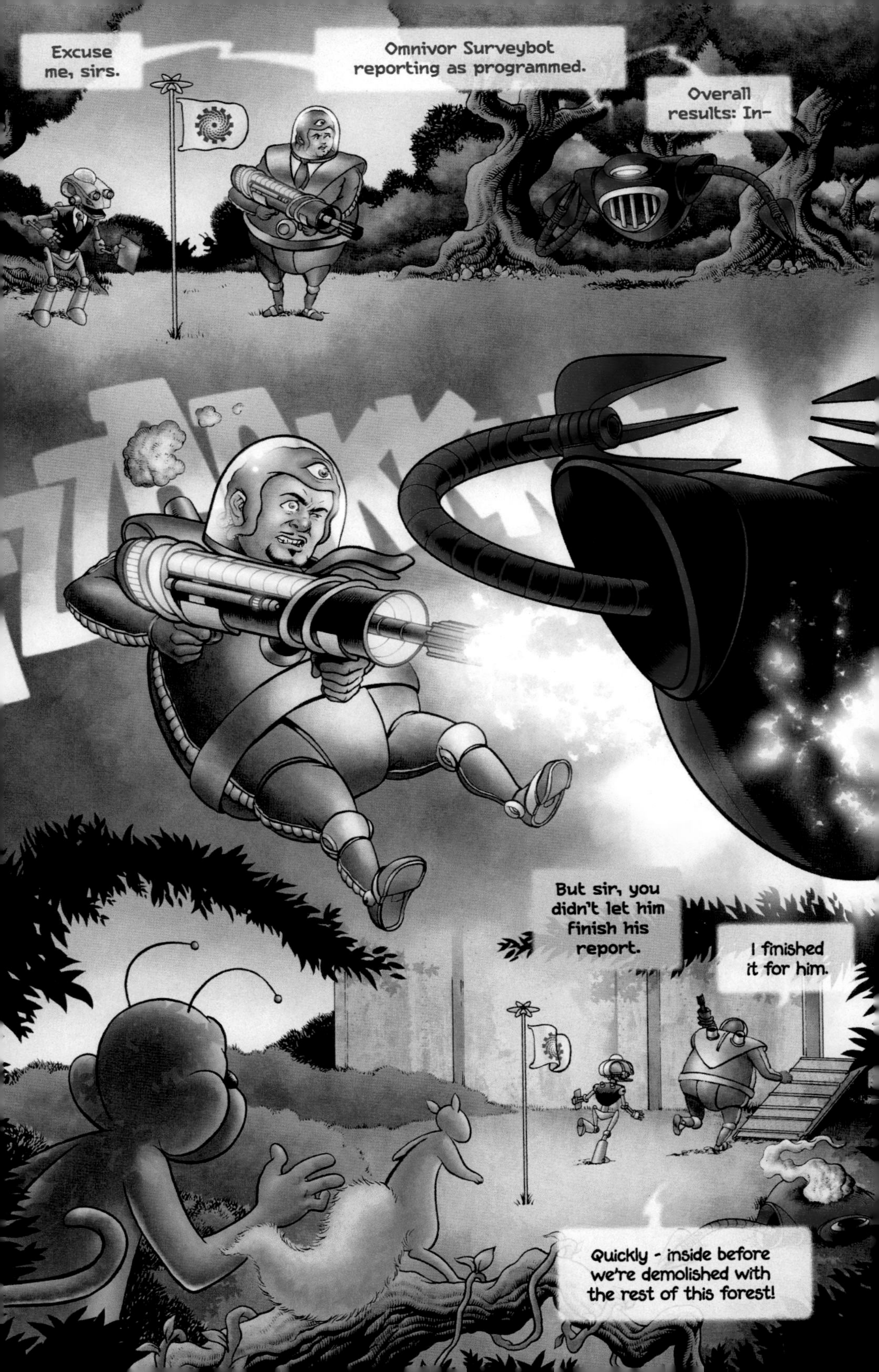
Excuse me, sirs.
Omnivor Surveybot reporting as programmed.
Overall results: In-
But sir, you didn't let him finish his report.
I finished it for him.
Quickly - inside before we're demolished with the rest of this forest!

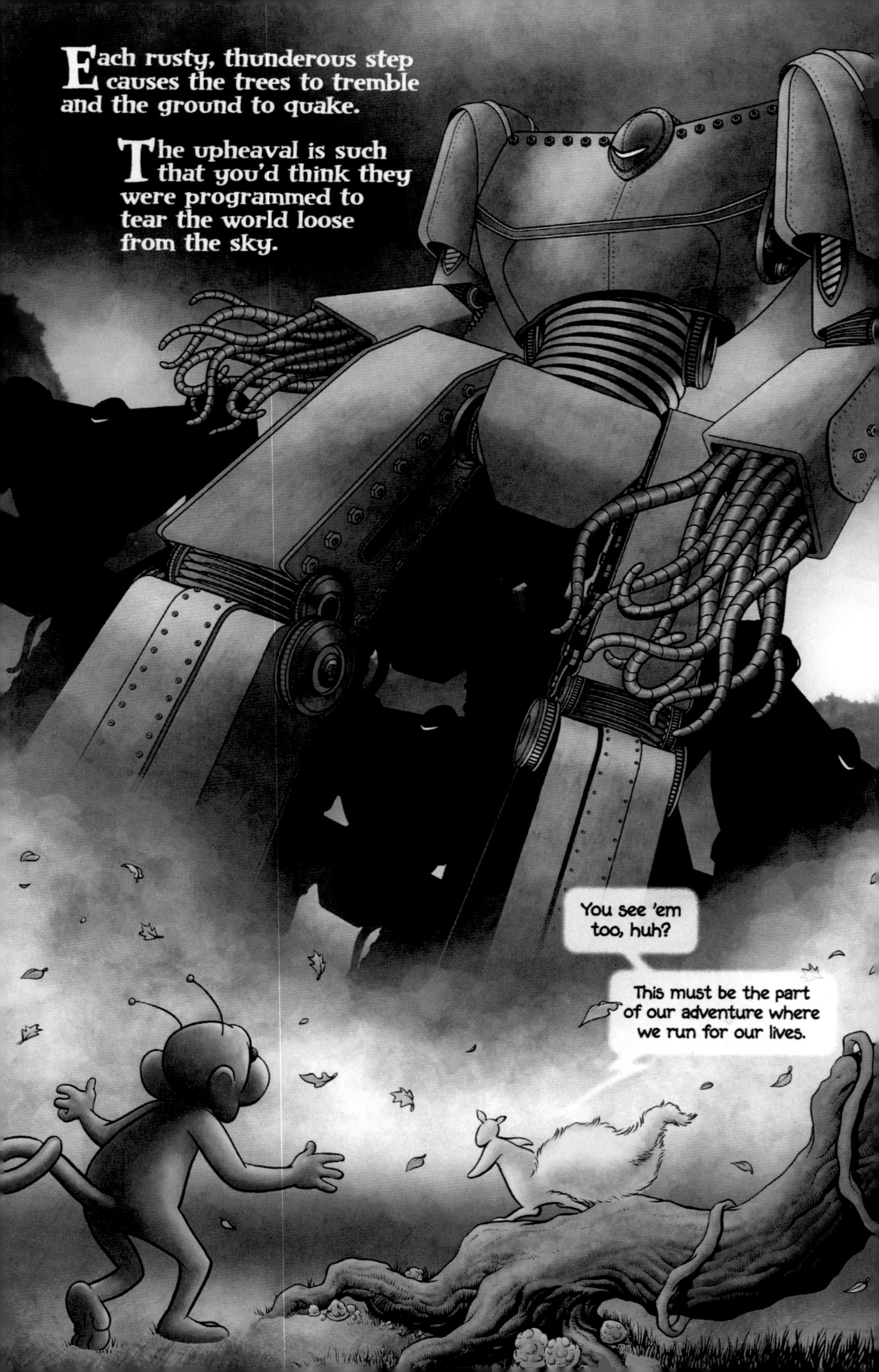
Each rusty, thunderous step causes the trees to tremble and the ground to quake.
The upheaval is such that you'd think they were programmed to tear the world loose from the sky.
You see 'em too, huh?
This must be the part of our adventure where we run for our lives.

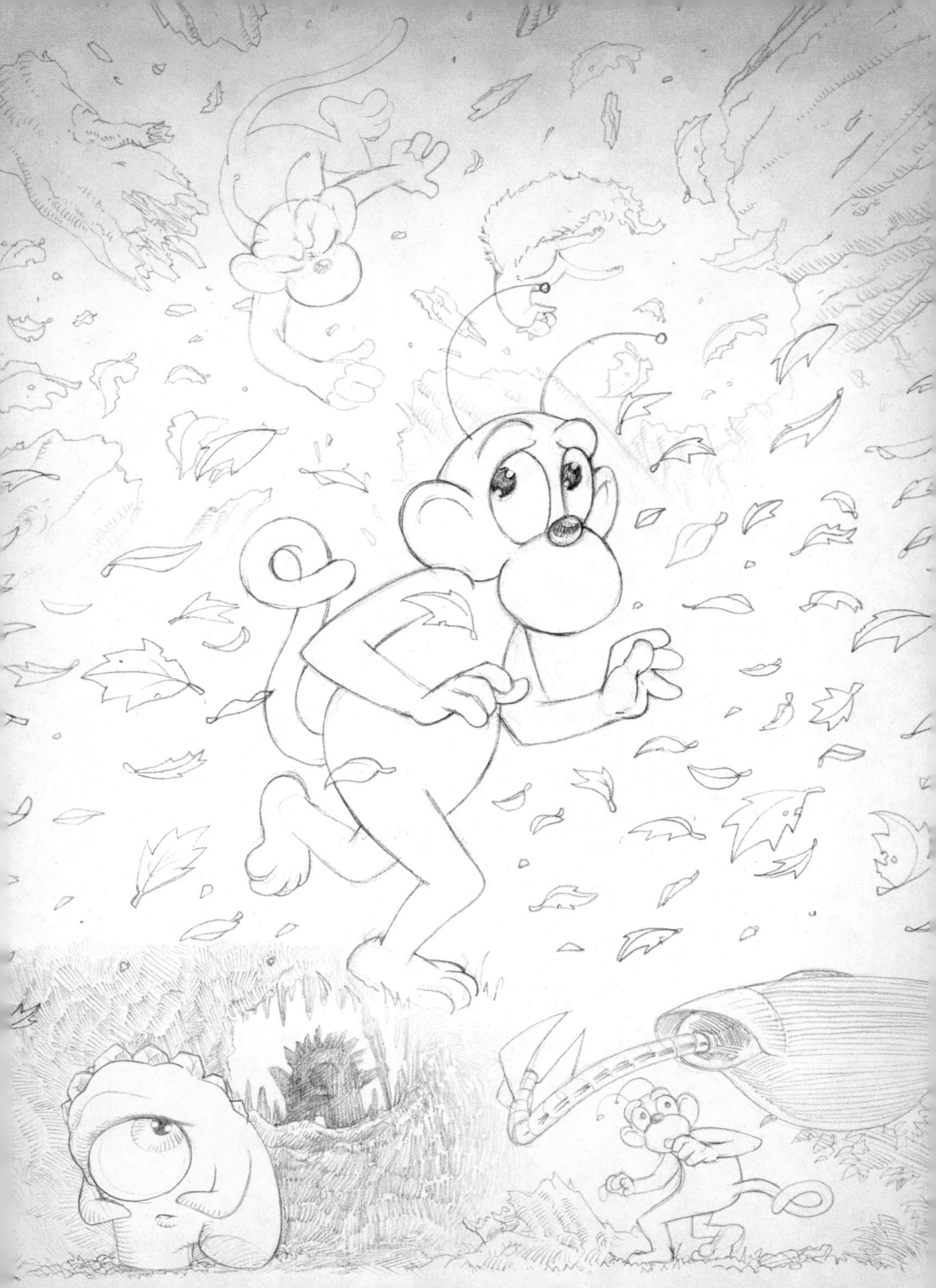

COMING UP NEXT IN BLOOP: PART TWO AND ONLINE AT BLOOPTHESPACEMONKEY.COM

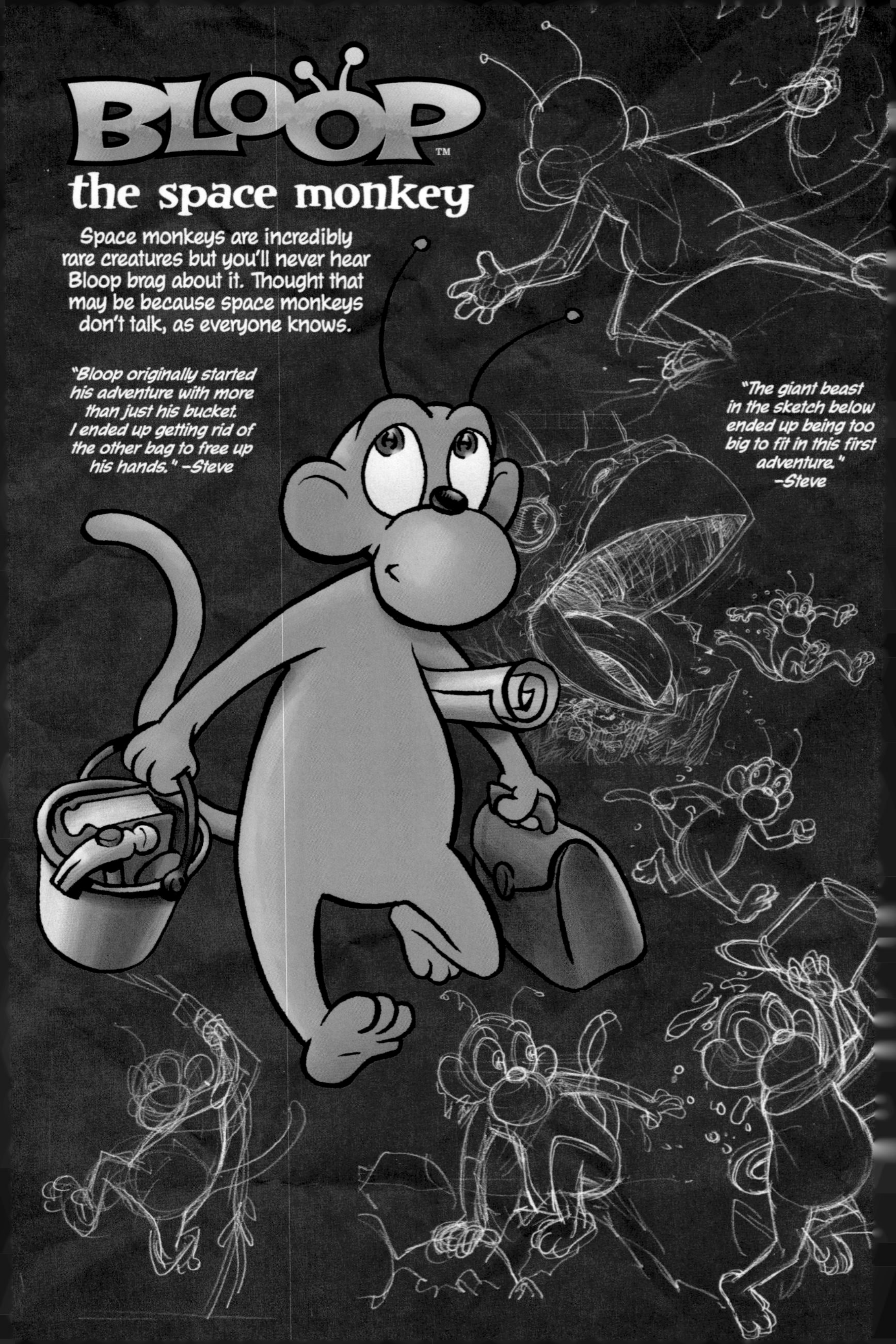
BLOOP™
the space monkey
Space monkeys are incredibly rare creatures but you'll never hear Bloop brag about it. Thought that may be because space monkeys don't talk, as everyone knows.
"Bloop originally started his adventure with more than just his bucket. I ended up getting rid of the other bag to free up his hands." –Steve
"The giant beast in the sketch below ended up being too big to fit in this first adventure." –Steve

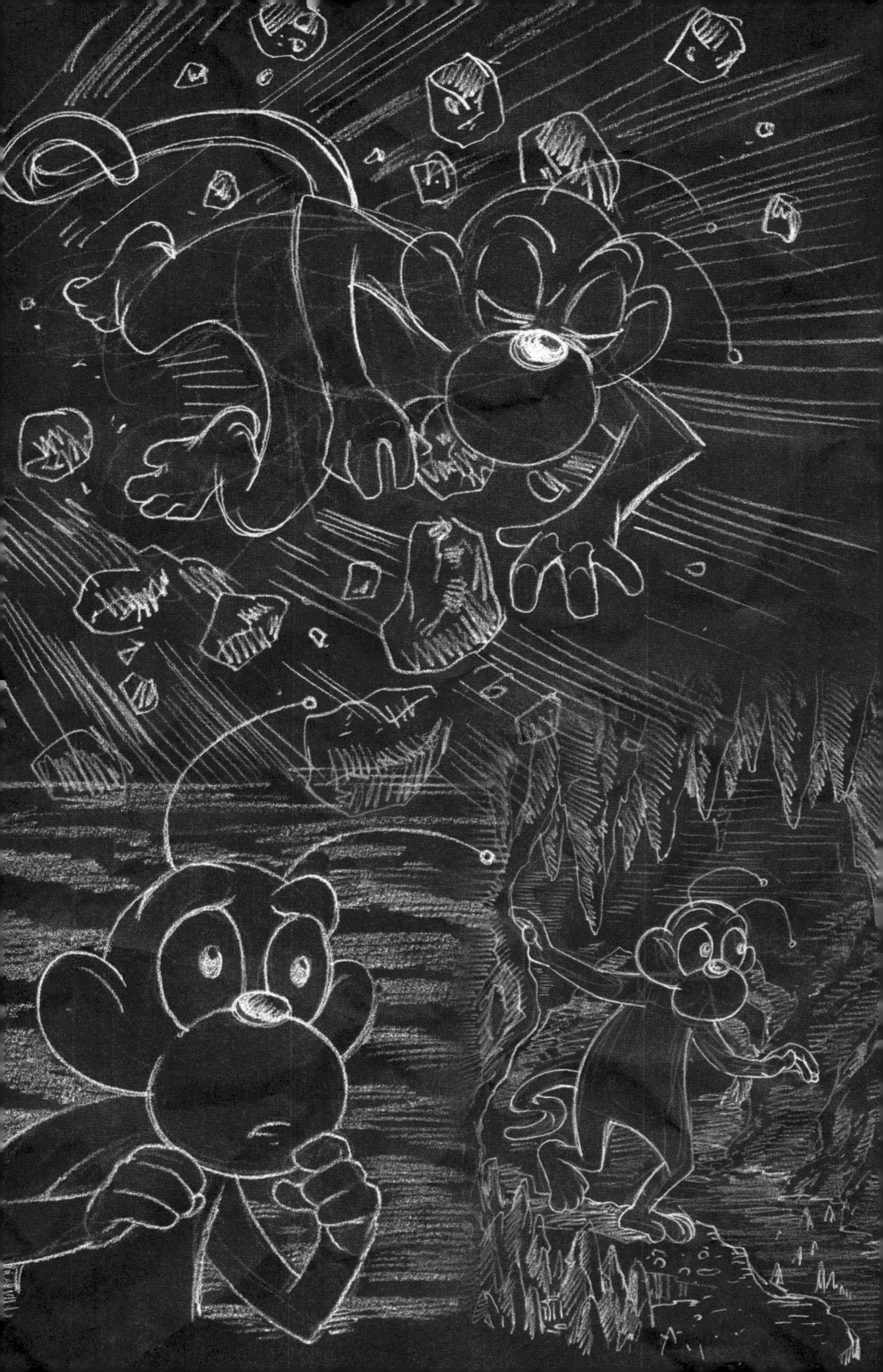

TOMO™
the critter

Bloop's friend Tomo believes he is not only the star of this adventure, but the star of every adventure. Tomo's dream is to be the greatest needlepoint artist in the history of the universe. Ever.

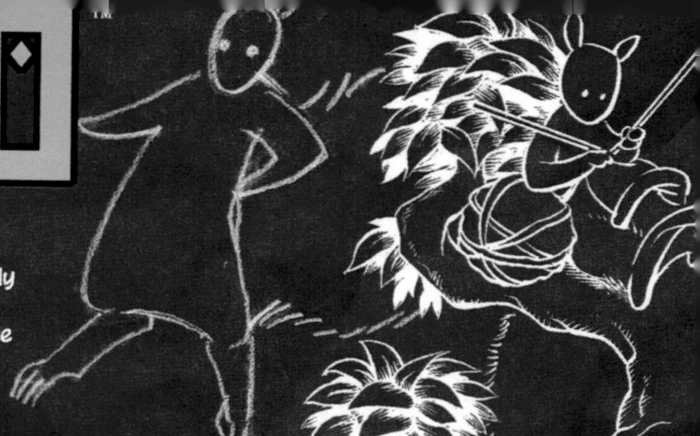

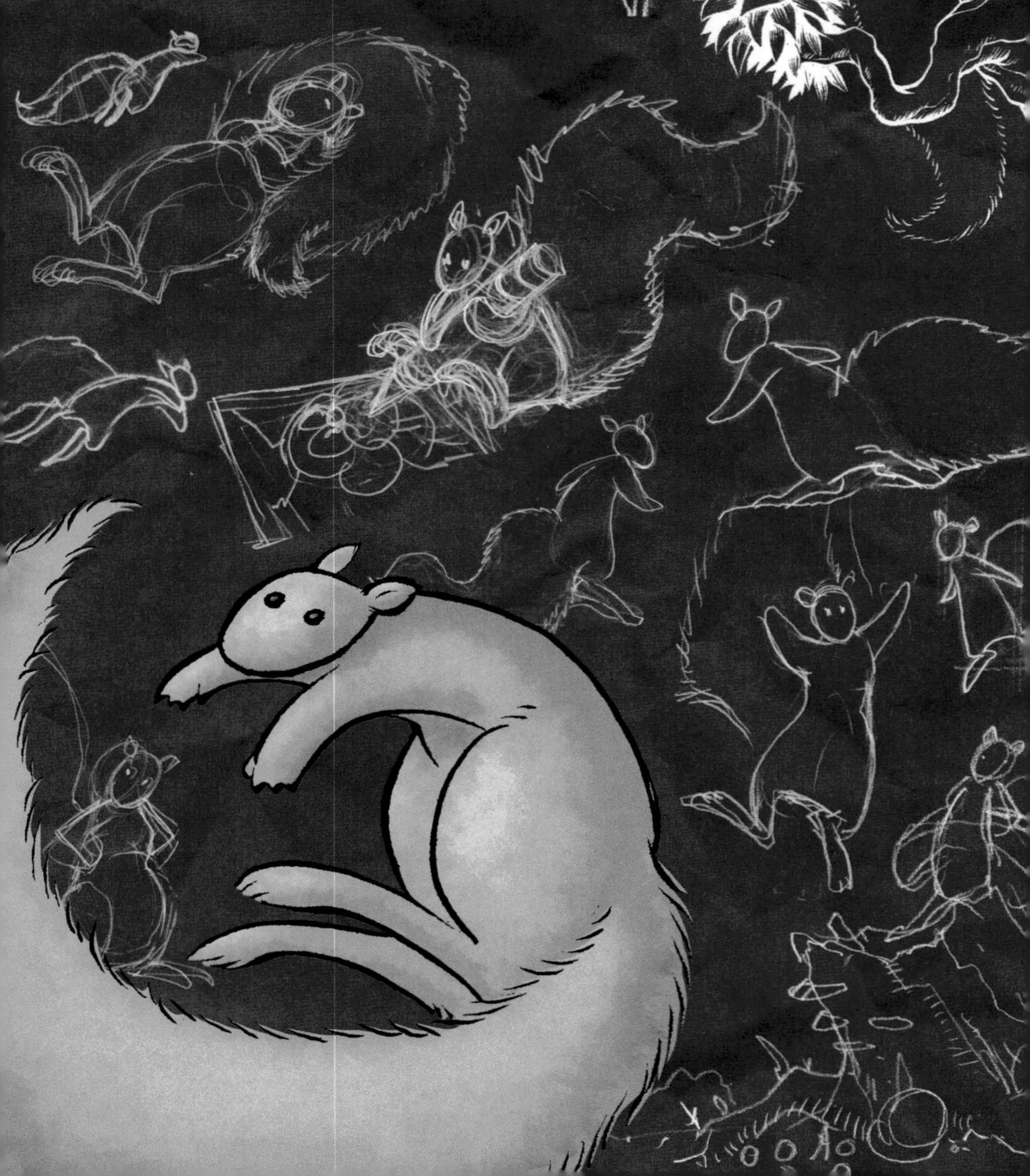

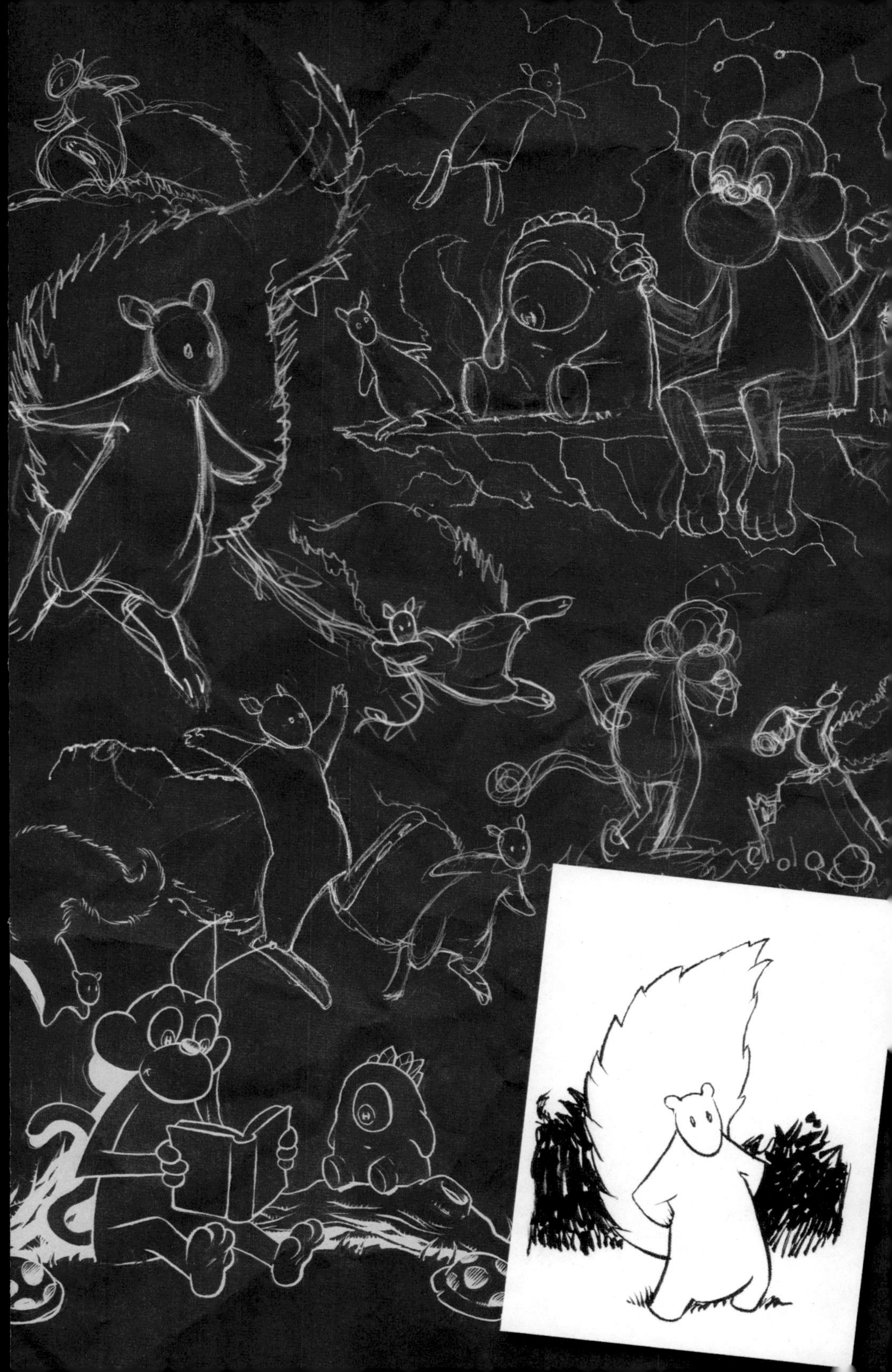

GLOM™

the... umm...

As of the first book, Bloop has only just seen Glom from a distance. Glom ran off with Bloop's book and pencil and then... disappeared.

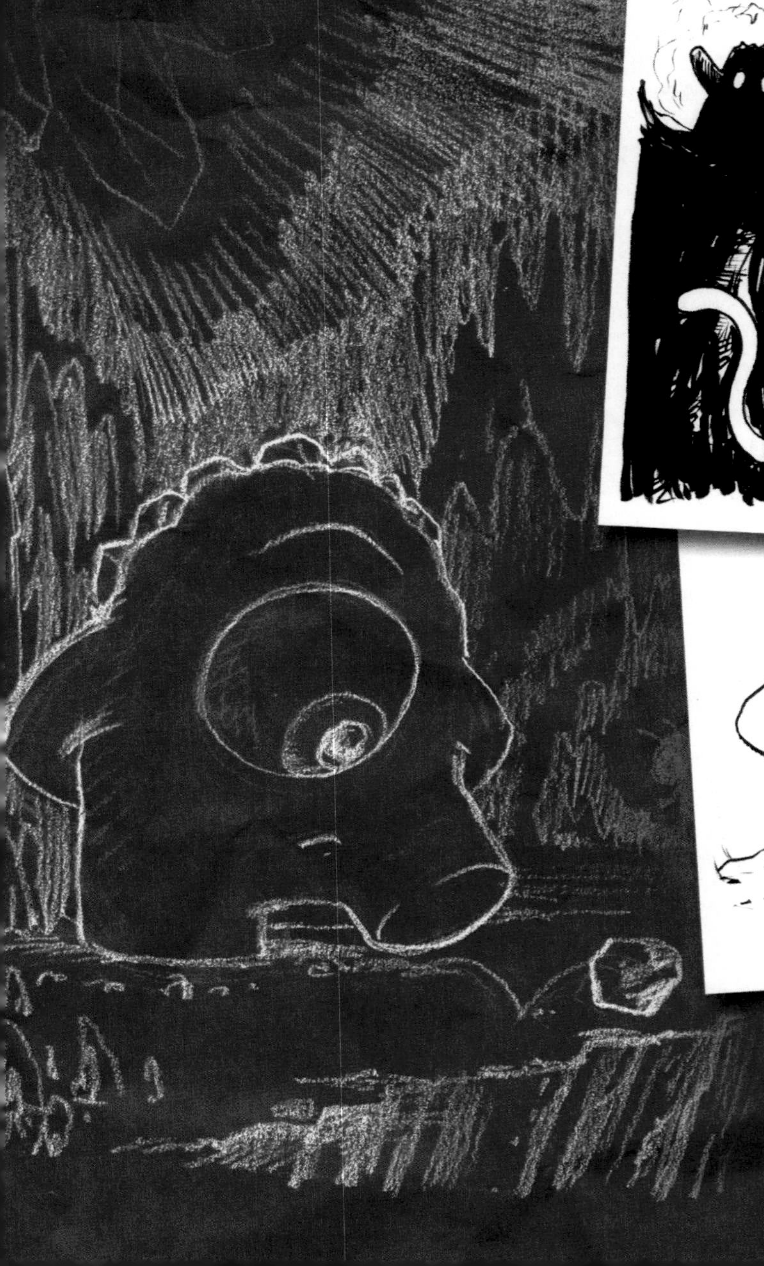

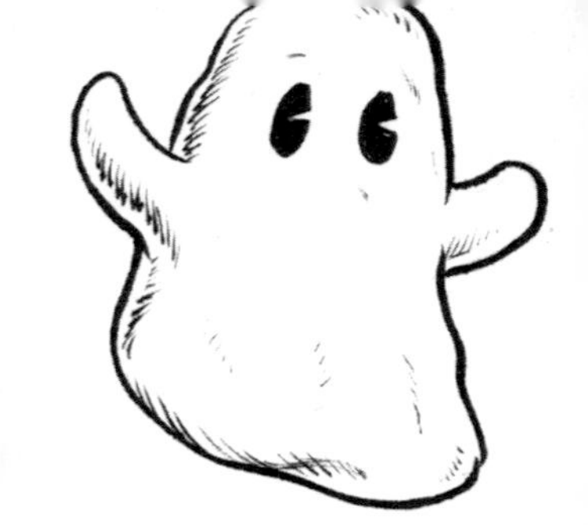

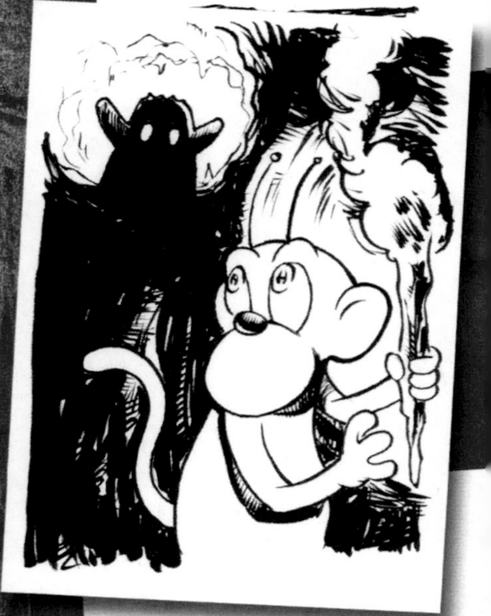

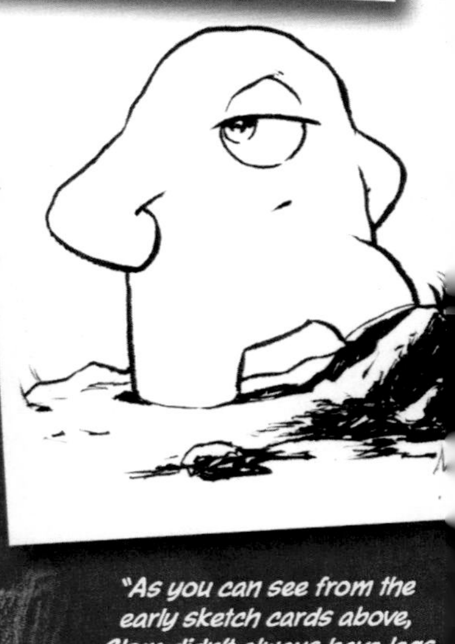

"As you can see from the early sketch cards above, Glom didn't always have legs in the early designs. He also didn't have the crystals growing from his head either."
–Steve

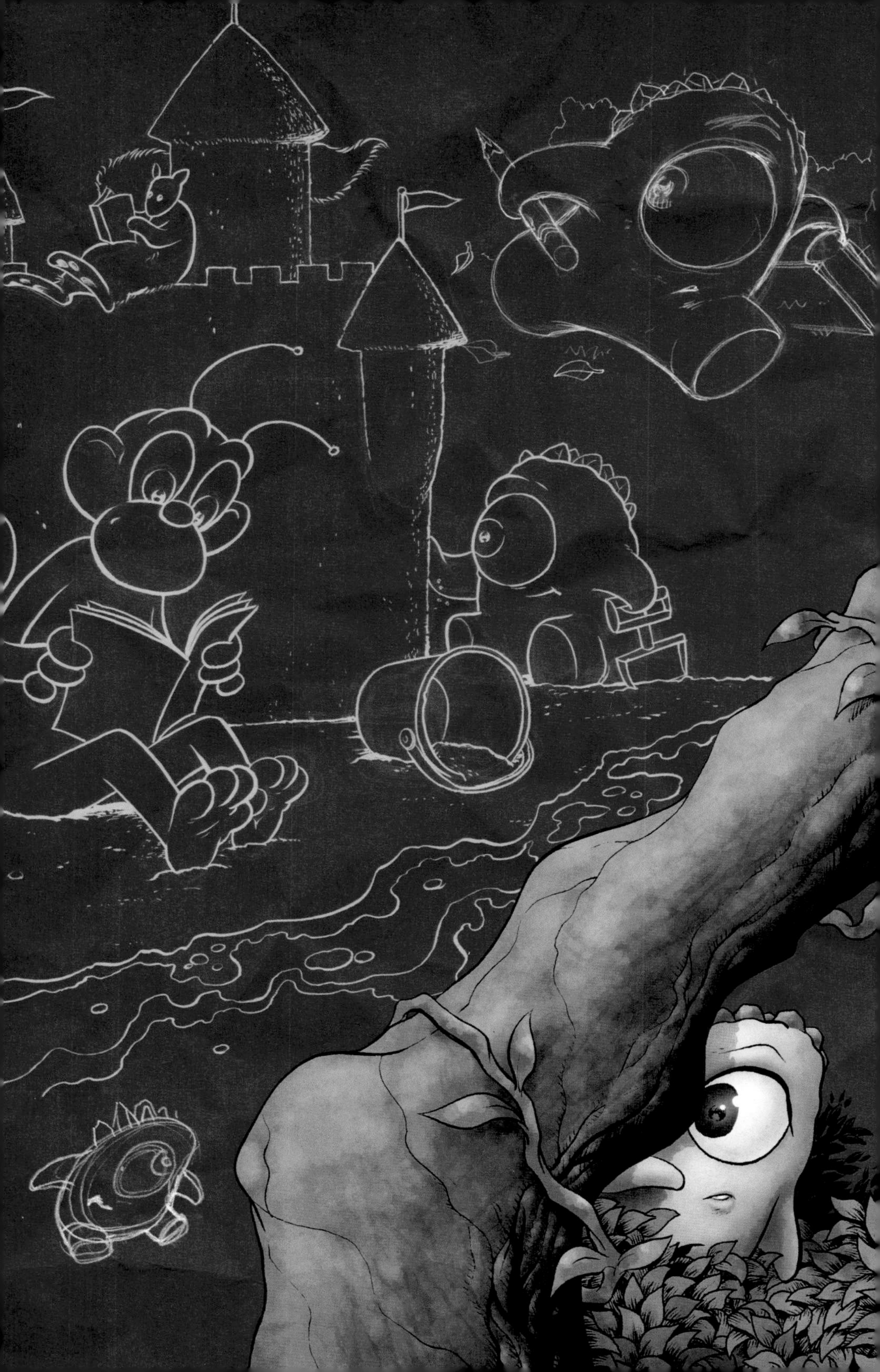

MINOR PINION™

the mid-level regional associate managerial administrator

Minor Pinion would tell you he loves his job but you wouldn't believe him. He doesn't believe him either. Pinion has a genetically-engineered squid stuck to his head which does not increase his intelligence like he thought it would.

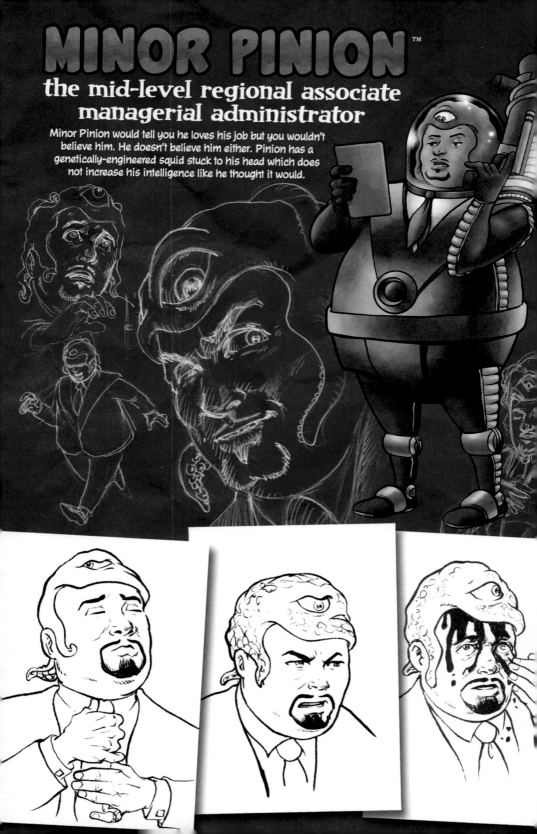

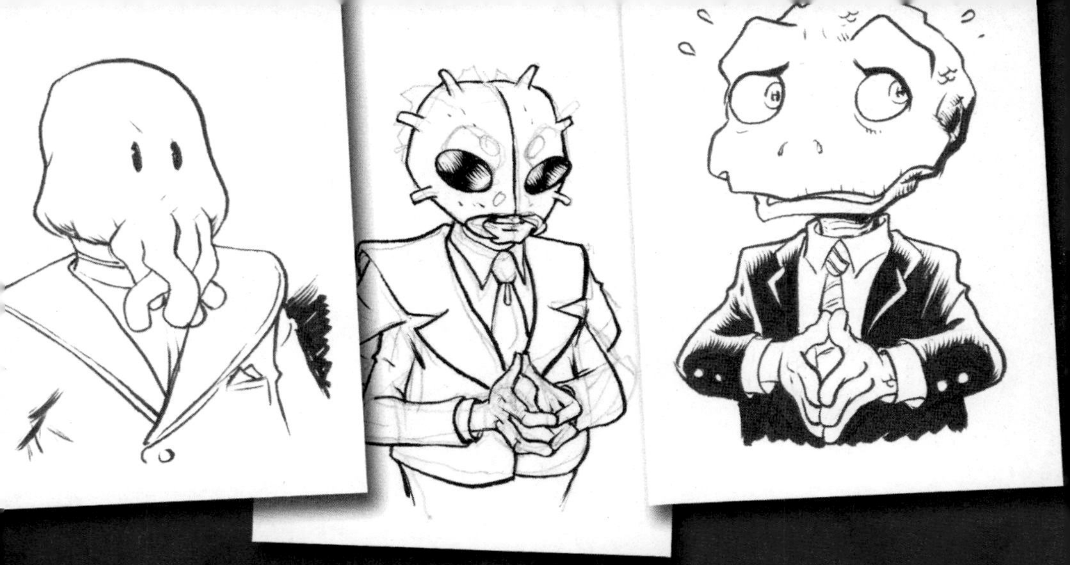

PINION'S ASSISTANTS & ROBOTS

In the challenging job market of the future, many qualified alien life forms applied for the job of Assistant to the Mid-Level Regional Associate Managerial Administrator at Omnivor Mining and Minerals, Inc.
Only one robot, Cogswell, was willing to work for so little pay.

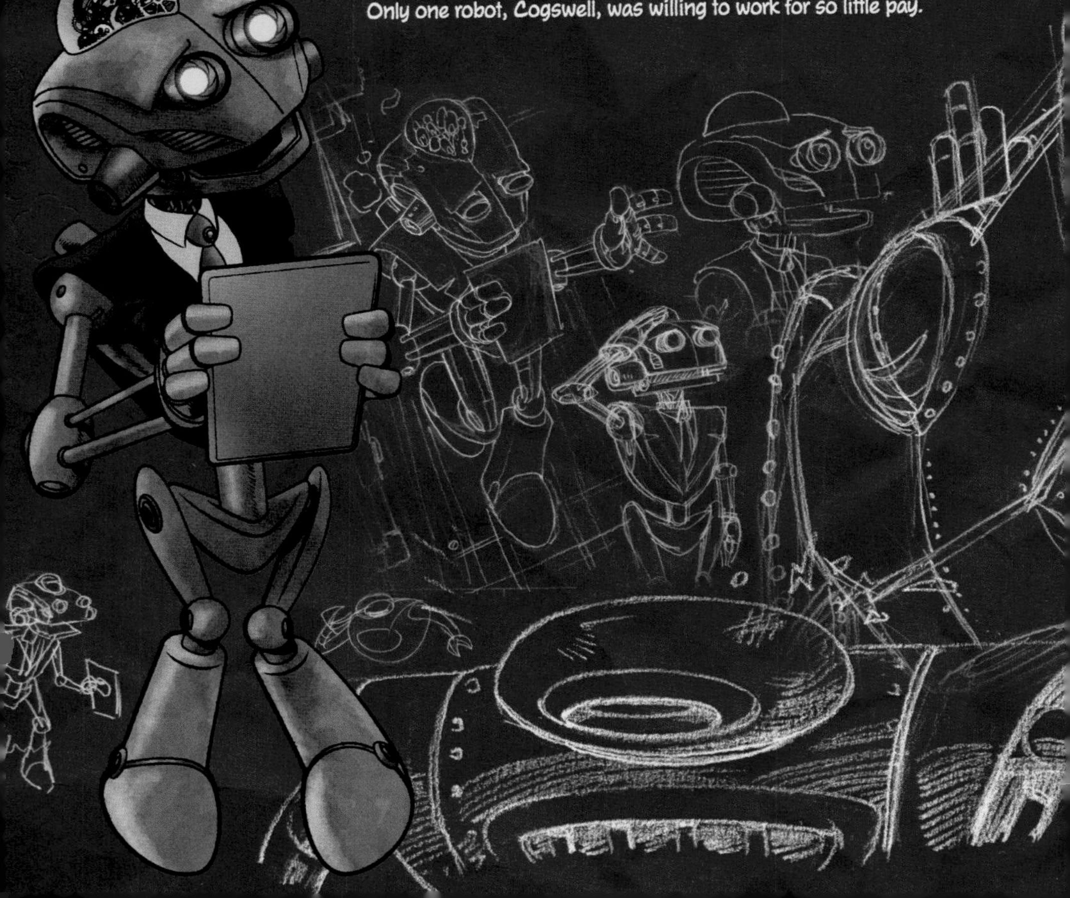

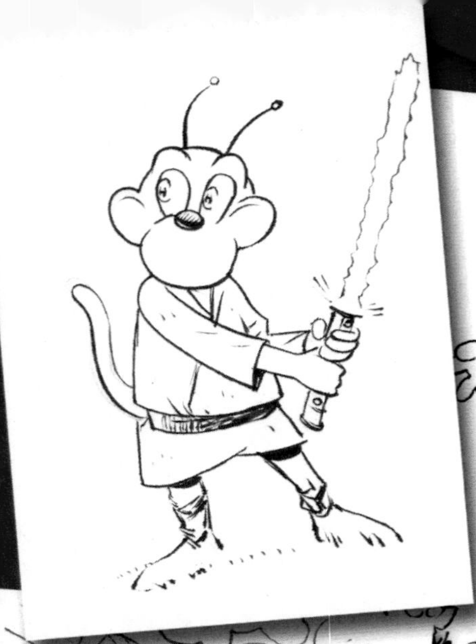
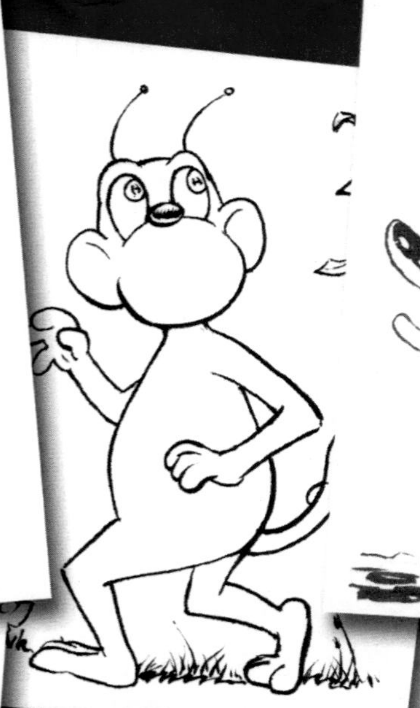
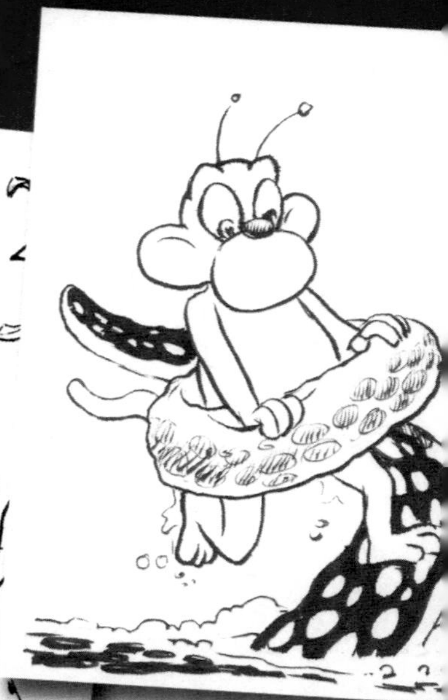
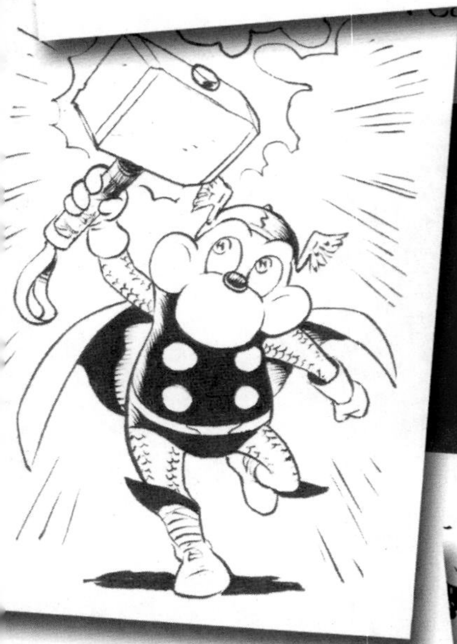

SKETCH CARDS

"Shown here are a few of the hundreds of sketch cards I've drawn at conventions over the past few years. These are always fun to do!" –Steve

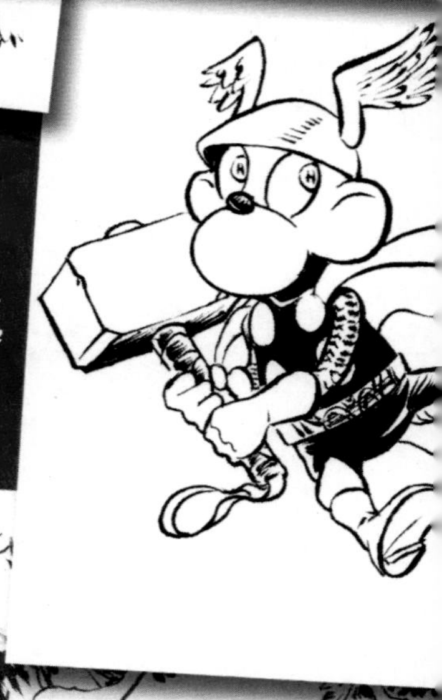
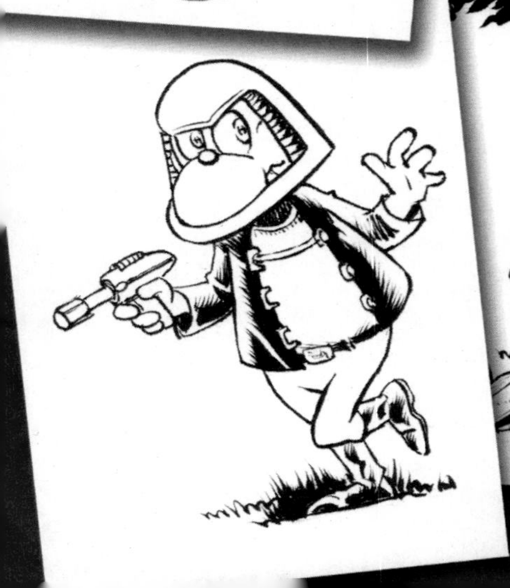
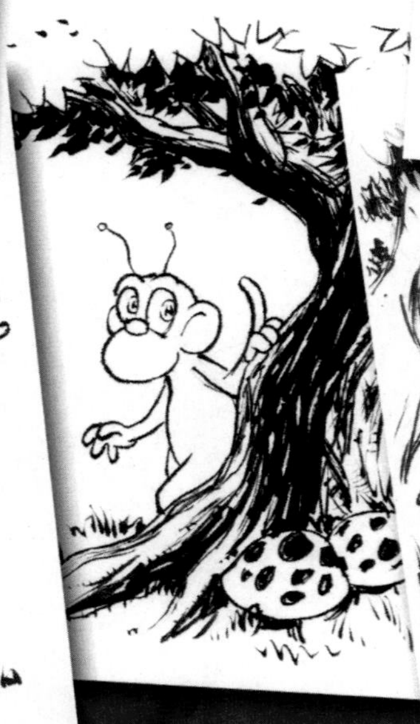
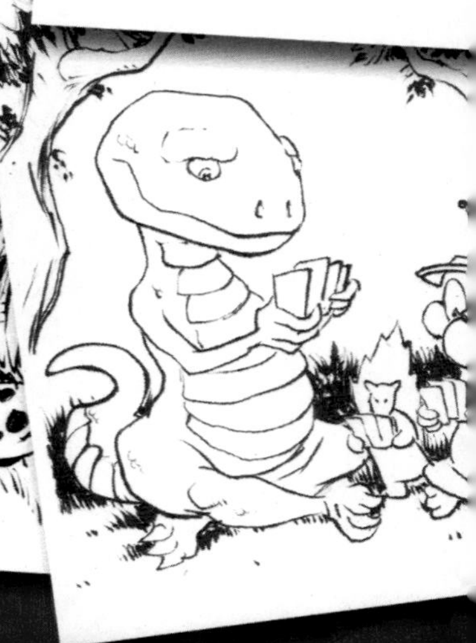

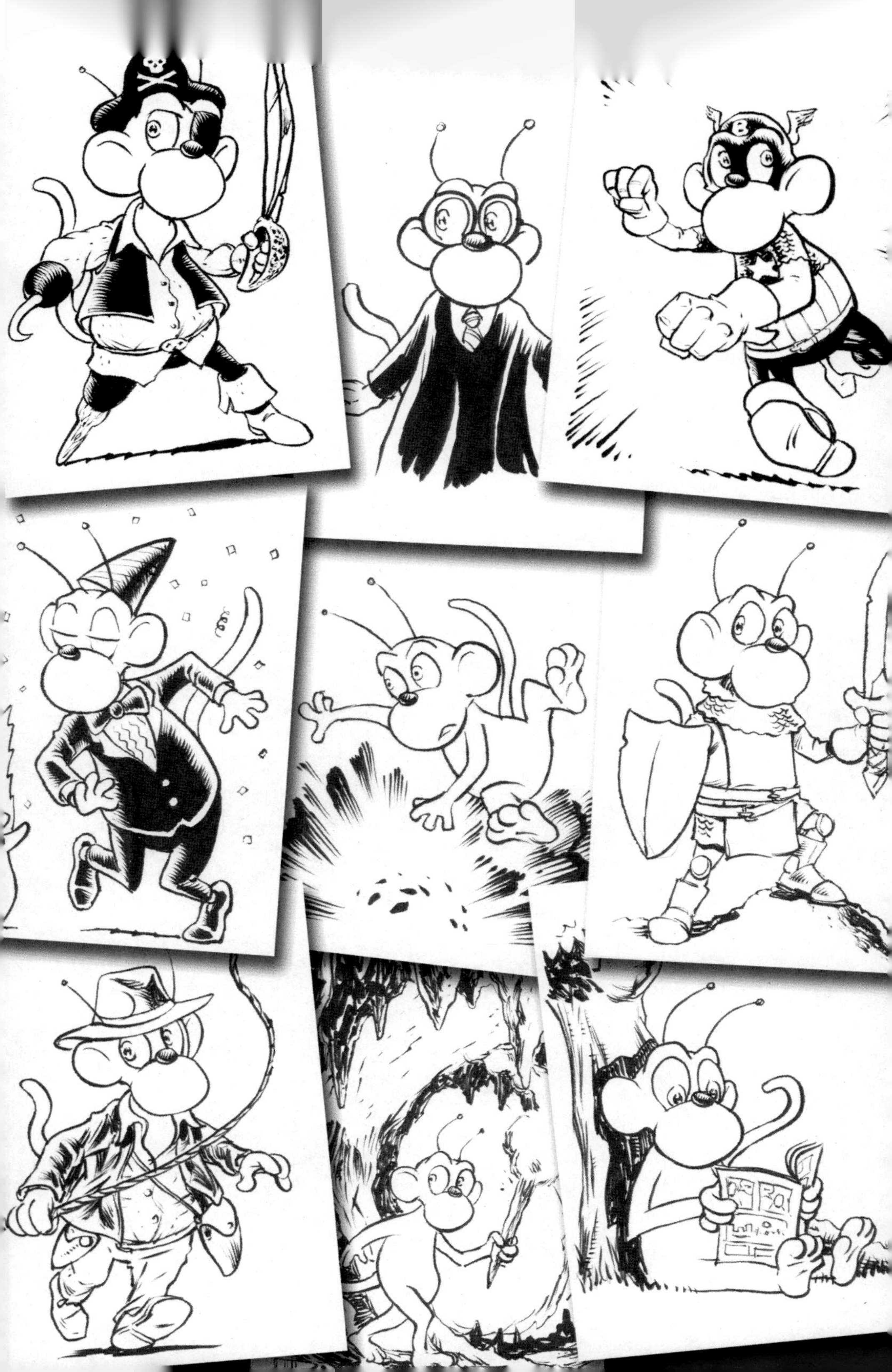

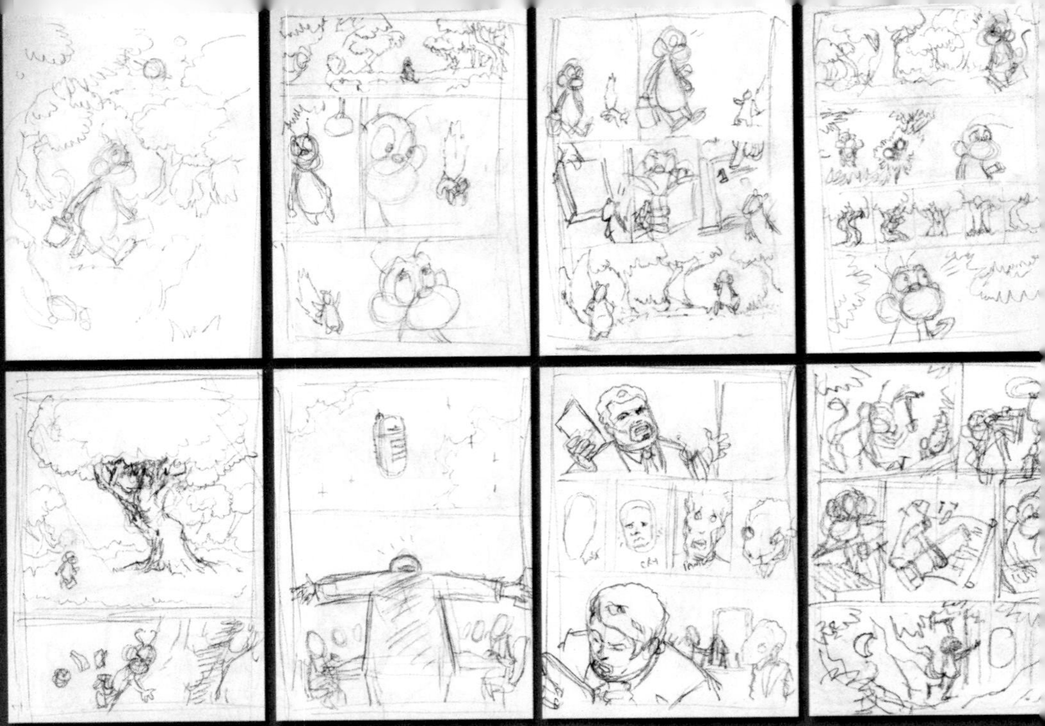

STORY "THUMB NAILS"

When planning a large graphic novel like Bloop, cartoonists often create small sketches of each page to plan the story. The eight "thumb nail" drawings seen here were each roughly the size of trading cards. If you look closely and compare them to the final pages, you can see that even with all the planning, many scenes changed completely.

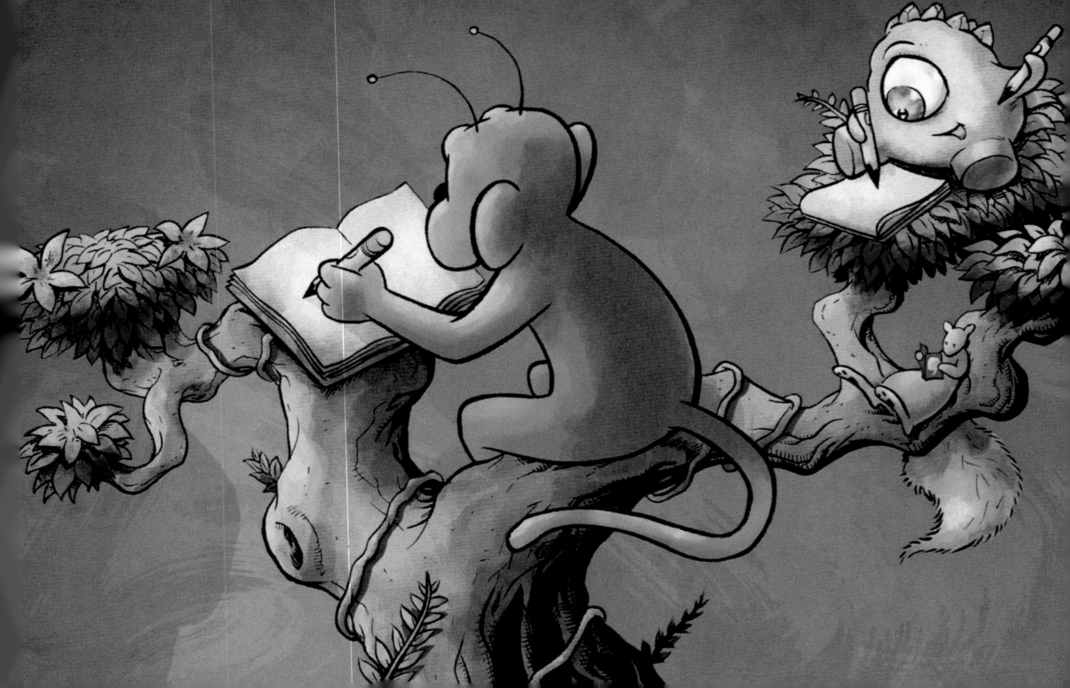

OMNIVOR'S POSTERS

f you look closely at the scenes in Pinion's office, you can see "retro"-style posters hanging on the walls "covering the mold."

These silly props were added to help make Pinion's office that much more depressing and to hint at just how bad it is to work for *Omnivor Minerals and Mining.*

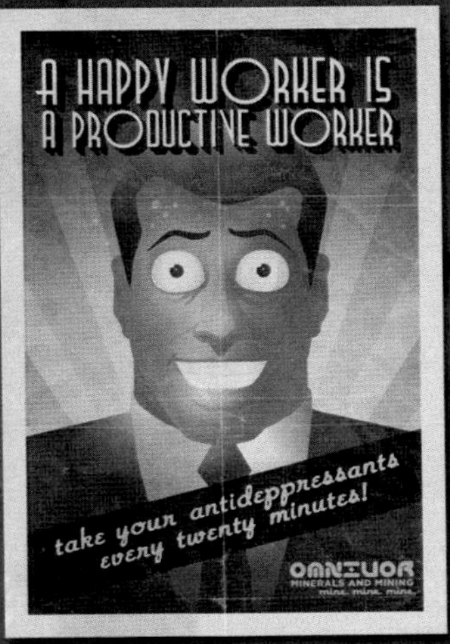
A HAPPY WORKER IS
A PRODUCTIVE WORKER
take your antidepressants
every twenty minutes!
OMNIVOR
MINERALS AND MINING
mine. mine. mine.

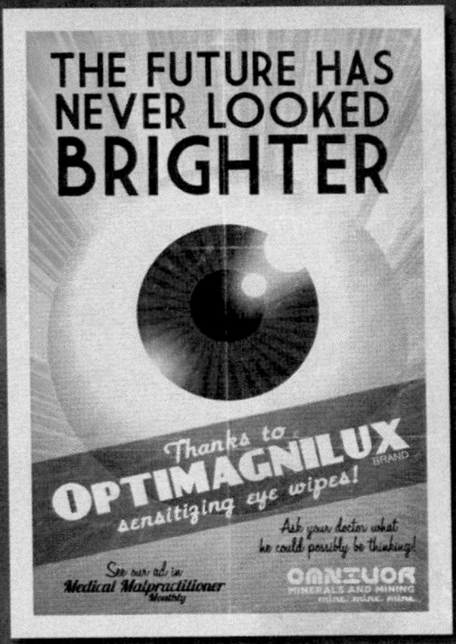
THE FUTURE HAS
NEVER LOOKED
BRIGHTER
Thanks to
OPTIMAGNILUX
sensitizing eye wipes!
Ask your doctor what
he could possibly be thinking!
See our ad in
Medical Malpractitioner
OMNIVOR
MINERALS AND MINING
mine. mine. mine.

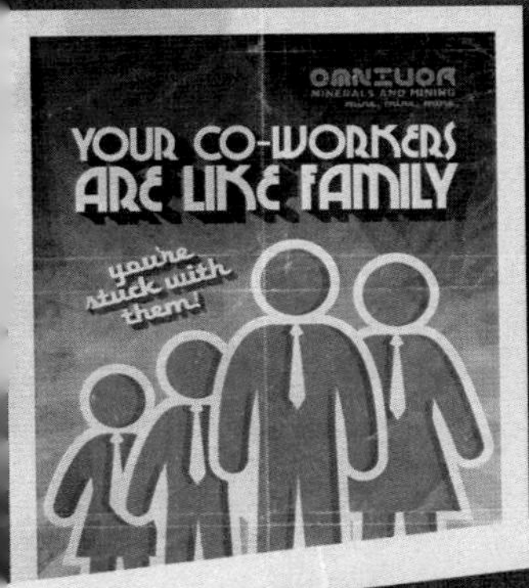
OMNIVOR
MINERALS AND MINING
mine. mine. mine.
YOUR CO-WORKERS
ARE LIKE FAMILY
you're
stuck with
them!

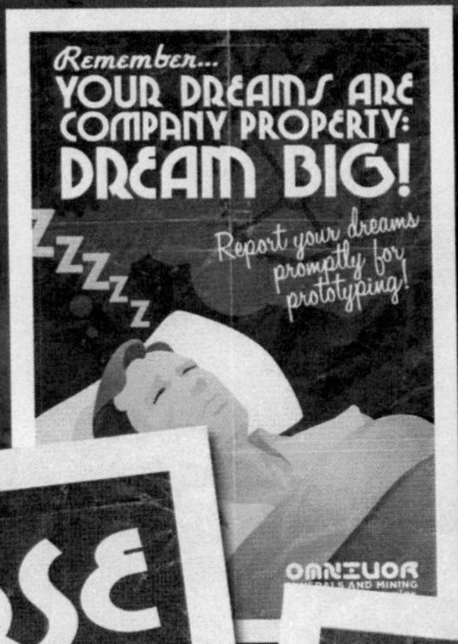
Remember...
YOUR DREAMS ARE
COMPANY PROPERTY:
DREAM BIG!
Report your dreams
promptly for
prototyping!
ZZZZZ
OMNIVOR
MINERALS AND MINING

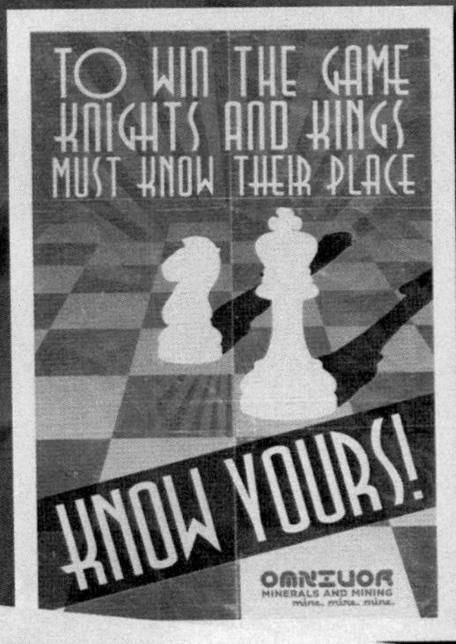
TO WIN THE GAME
KNIGHTS AND KINGS
MUST KNOW THEIR PLACE
KNOW YOURS!
OMNIVOR
MINERALS AND MINING
mine. mine. mine.

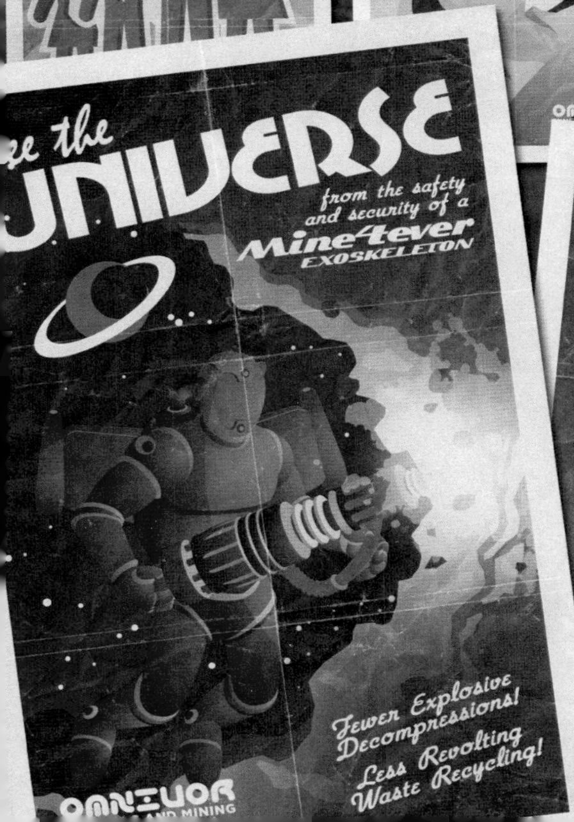
e the
UNIVERSE
from the safety
and security of a
Mine4ever
EXOSKELETON
Fewer Explosive
Decompressions!
Less Revolting
Waste Recycling!
OMNIVOR
AND MINING

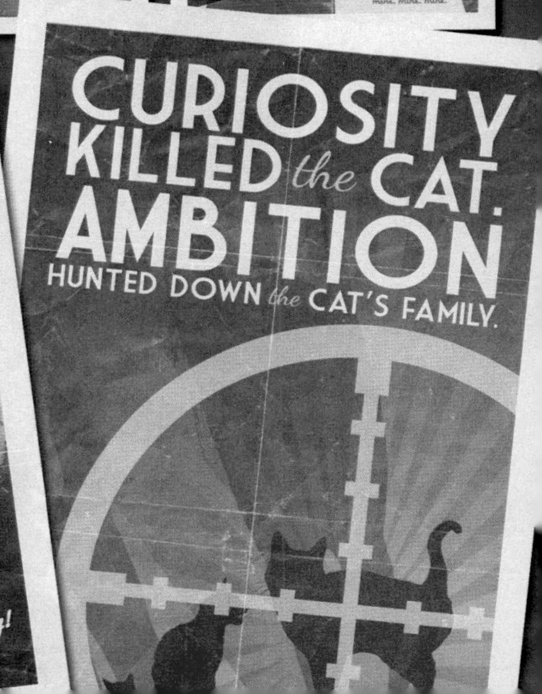
CURIOSITY
KILLED the CAT.
AMBITION
HUNTED DOWN the CAT'S FAMILY.

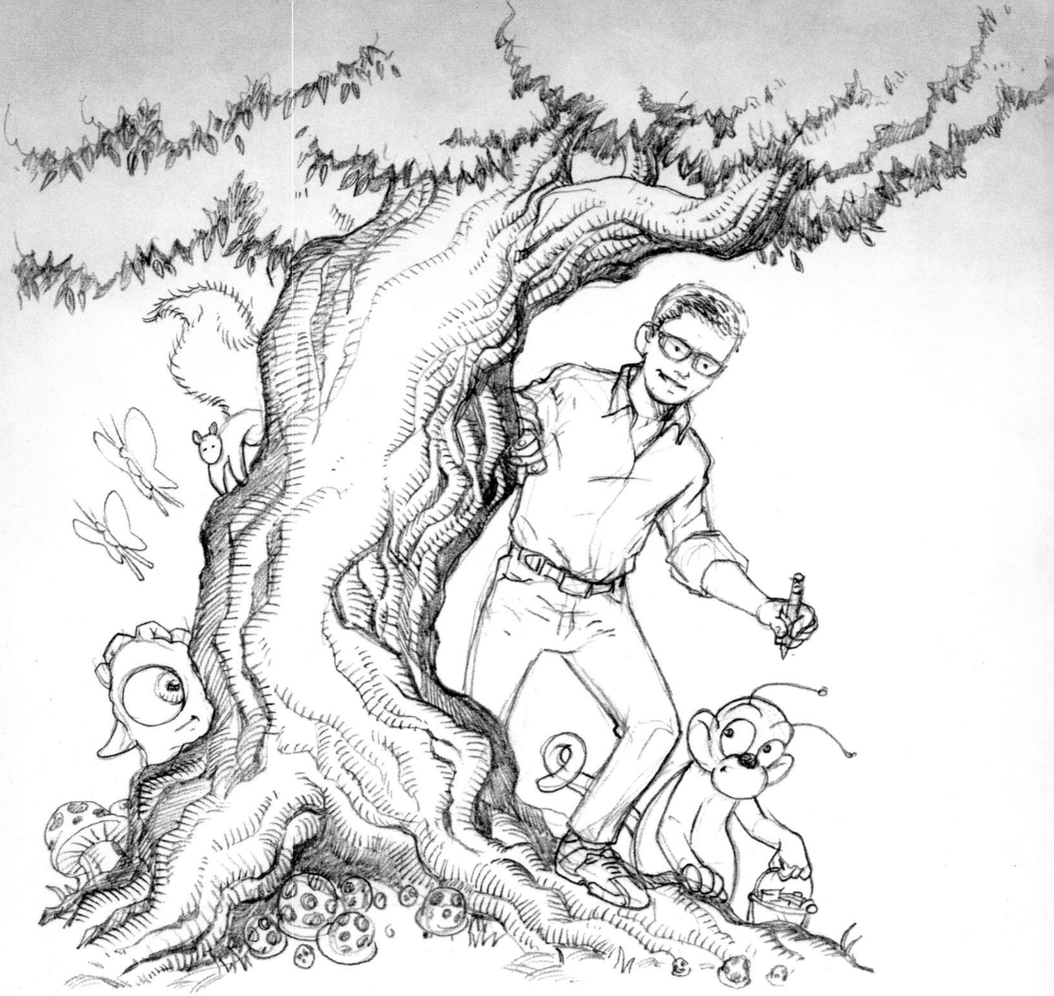

About the Cartoonist

Steve Conley is the writer and artist of dozens of comics and web comics including *Star Trek: Year Four*, *Michael Chabon presents The Amazing Adventures of the Escapist*, *Aquaman* and many others.

Steve has received nominations for cartooning's highest honors including The Will Eisner Comic Industry Award and The Harvey Award. Steve won the british Eagle Award for his fan-favorite, science-fiction series *Astounding Space Thrills*.

Steve's other cartoon creations include *The Kid Knight*, *The Other Kids*, *Socks and Barney*, *The Middle Age*, and *Jack Galaxy in the 21st Century*.

Steve currently lives on a beautiful, green planet circling a yellow star.

www.bloopthespacemonkey.com